Taking a Long Shot

Taking a Long Shot

Taking a Long Shot

Love, Life and Peril in Wartime Vietnam

by
Dave Cassier

DCO Books

Taking a Long Shot:
Love, Life and Peril in Wartime Vietnam
Copyright © Dave Cassier, 2023
1st Edition 2023
First Published 2023

DCO Books
This edition published by
Proglen Trading Co., Ltd.
Bangkok Thailand
http://www.dco.co.th

Contents

Preface

The US government made use of thousands of civilian contractors during the Vietnam War. These people were hired by companies that had contracts with the US military, and they were indispensable to its efforts there. They did all sorts of work … logistics, training, depot and warehouse operation, construction, piloting aircraft, maintenance … the list went on. As in all war zones, there were no safe places, so taking the risk was rewarded with lucrative salaries.

For most, taking a job in a hostile area is a pivotal decision, and they seldom go back to the lives they once lived. For many contractors, it's their first visit to another country, and this is the story of one such unprepared young man.

Most of what is described in the following pages is based upon actual events, although the chronology and the names of people and certain organizations have been altered.

Chapter 1

March 29, 2020; Lancaster, California

Jake Kendell swung his F-150 pickup truck into the gravel driveway of his mother's old double-wide mobile home, and parked next to a new sedan that he didn't recognize. Trees were flowering nicely; her garden was all yellow, blue, and red blooms. Jake made it a point to visit his mom, Clara, every week or two since he had retired from the US Army back in 2010, but in recent years he would always be there on March 29, Vietnam Veterans' Day.

His mother greeted him at the door with a cup of coffee. She was a large woman who had a cherubic, healthy look about her, which belied her 77 years.

"Jake…. Give your mom a hug…. Jenny's here already. She's got a new car. Nice isn't it."

Jake and his younger sister, Jenny, had quite a few things in common. Both were into the tail-end of middle-age, and retired from the military – he a US Army master sergeant, she a staff sergeant. They were both out of shape, and both were twice divorced with extended families of children and step-children, most of whom they didn't see much of.

On the kitchen wall, Clara displayed a framed photo of their father, Wade, in Vietnam, smiling, with his long hair combed back, wearing a T-shirt and a shoulder-holstered pistol.

Jake remembered more about his father than Jenny did, although he was only five years old when Wade went away. He knew that his dad had been an auto mechanic, and could recall him coming home after work each day, tall and wiry, in stained coveralls, going immediately to the refrigerator for a cold beer before doing anything else. There were fleeting memories of Wade sitting on the porch steps, watching Jake and the other neighborhood kids playing football in the street. Wade would sit and drink his beer without ever coaching from the sidelines, without ever throwing a pass or taking a catch.

As Jake and Jenny drank their coffee at the kitchen table and reminisced about their Army days, Clara served fresh buttered pancakes. They each took a helping and poured maple syrup over it. Clara was happy whenever her son and daughter would visit like this. Last year, they had to call off the visit to the cemetery because the weather was so bad and Jenny had a cold, but today was bright and crisp, and Clara had bought flowers ready for the occasion.

Jake and Jenny finished their coffee and got up from the table, ready to go. As she put on her jacket, Clara's thoughts were already drifting off to Wade and when he went away to Vietnam, so long ago....

Chapter 2

November 11, 1968; Ho Nai, Dong Nai Province, Vietnam

The bus rolled up to the security gate shortly before 7:00 a.m. and stopped to allow the Vietnamese passengers to get out and pass through the checkpoint, one by one. It was like a civilian version of a school bus, and was one of the transport vehicles for Atlantic Architect & Engineers. The Vietnamese that rode the bus were not laborers, of whom there were hundreds at the location; rather, they were office staff, storekeepers, or skilled workers. Wade Kendell and the other foreigners on the bus weren't considered security risks; they simply grabbed their things, got off, and walked the short distance to the operations building, which was a large, hastily-constructed prefab covered in dust that continually whipped up from the red soil found in much of Vietnam. At the ops building, the foreigners signed in, read any new notices posted on the bulletin board, and went off to their work stations.

As Kendell strode over to the equipment motor pool in Area 208, he watched two young Vietnamese office girls gliding along in their flowing white *áo dài* dresses, split at the sides, with black pantaloons underneath. They held hands while walking, and wore the traditional *nón lá*, the conical straw hat. Kendell thought the same thing he did every time he saw them: there was nothing so exquisite back in Lancaster, California, and they seemed so out of place in this barren, dusty outpost.

Area 208 was 23 acres of open storage for engineering materials. There were yards filled with tons of bridge timbers, perforated landing mats for aircraft runways, steel beams, concertina wire, drums of asphalt, bulk cement, portable bridges, and tanks of acetylene and oxygen. All of it required heavy equipment to handle and move, and Kendell had a crew of local workers who maintained the dozens of forklifts, cranes, trucks, buses, and jeeps owned by the company.

At the motor pool workshop, Kendell's supervisor, Ralph Gates, greeted him. "Hey, Wade, how you doing?"

"Okay, Ralph. How are you?"

But, in fact, Kendell wasn't feeling all that great. The previous night, he'd bought a case of Falstaff beer at the post exchange, and drank most of it while his girlfriend finished just one can. Ralph knew that Wade was hungover, but the guy always showed up and did his job.

Kendell headed straight for the water cooler and gulped down a big cupful. He then took a clipboard from the wall, which had all his work orders for the day.

Somehow he managed to get most of the jobs done each day. This surprised him, because some of his men were getting long in the tooth. Kendell had soon found out the reason for this. The company could not employ any military-aged men. South Vietnam required total conscription of all males between the ages of 18 and 45 years. So, Area 208 was mostly staffed by young, educated Vietnamese women in the office, hundreds of women from Ho Nai village who were laborers in the yards, and the older men doing the repair work in the shops – which they mostly did well.

As he did each morning, Kendell assigned his mechanics to their repair and maintenance tasks, then retreated into the air-conditioned office, where he often spent time reflecting. Christ, what a stroke of luck, landing here. It kept him from being drafted into the Army, as the job was under a military contract. Back home, it was four bucks an hour, working his ass off in the Mobil station, mainly doing oil changes and brake jobs. Had he not stumbled upon that job fair in Bakersfield, he never would have known about AA&E. Clara wasn't keen on it at first, but when he told her he'd be making 1,800 bucks a month to start, tax free, she relented. It was very difficult raising two kids on his wages from the gas station.

Chapter 3

March 17, 1968; Saigon

Kendell had been apprehensive during the Pan-Am flight to Tan Son Nhat Airport, Saigon. He arrived mid-morning, and it took ages to clear customs and immigration. Passengers were packed into the arrival hall, processing was at a snail's pace, and the heat was heavy. He was concerned upon exiting the terminal with his luggage. There were masses of people, and he didn't know exactly what to do, as touts and taxi-drivers crowded around him. He felt relieved only when a chubby, neatly-dressed Vietnamese man appeared in front of him holding a sign, "AA&E," with Kendell's name written underneath.

"Mr. Kendell?"

Kendell nodded.

"My name Minh. I take you to your hotel."

Minh took Kendell's bags and led the way to a white Datsun sedan in the parking lot. With the luggage stowed in the trunk, they eased out into calamitous traffic.

Minh was talkative and friendly. "This your first time in Vietnam?"

"Yeah," replied Kendell.

"Mr. Kendell, you need to change money? I can do for you."

"Okay, after we get to the hotel."

They were on Cong Ly Street, headed downtown, and Kendell could hardly believe what he was seeing. Already he thought all this was going to take some getting used to. There were cars, military and civilian trucks, buses, bicycles, cyclo pedicabs, and a river of small motorcycles weaving all around them. Girls seemed to be driving most of the motorbikes, and Kendell was stunned that they were nearly all covered from head to toe – long sleeves, gloves, *nón lá*, and face bandanas – which seemed crazy to him in this heat. The constant beeping and honking of all this traffic was insane, and the smells from the street food stalls were overpowering and starting to get to him through the open window. Fish sauce, or *nuoc mam*, was used in just about every dish, as Minh explained.

Outside the Catinat Hotel, Minh squeezed the little Datsun into a spot among scores of parked motorcycles, and escorted Kendell into the lobby and waited while he checked in. Once that was done, Kendell joined Minh in the sitting area.

"How much money to change, Mr. Kendell?"

Kendell replied, "One hundred dollars."

"Okay, two hundred piastres for one dollar. So, twenty thousand."

"Sounds good to me," said Kendell.

In fact, Minh knew where to change this 100 bucks and get 24,000 piastres for it. The official rate was 118 piastres at the banks, but no one in Saigon ever changed money at banks.

Minh handed him a business card. "Mr. Kendell, anything you need, you call me. You want to rent a nice house … anything, I can help."

The hotel was on Tu Do Street, in the heart of Saigon, where things were happening. There were bars, nightclubs, restaurants, cafés, shops, and hotels in this lively area, so AA&E used the Catinat for new arrivals into the country. They could stay there, expenses paid, for up to two weeks, by which time they would have to arrange their own accommodation. The Catinat had its own lobby bar and café, and an elevator – which Kendell was relieved to hear, as he was allocated room 402.

Upstairs in his room, he was also glad that the air-conditioner was working well. He showered and laid on the bed. What he really wanted was to get a beer and look around, but it was only just after 2:00 p.m., and still too hot and early for that, so he closed his eyes and drifted off.

At 5:30, he was jolted by the harsh ringing of the bedside telephone. At first, he didn't know where he was, but it came back to him in a few seconds, and he picked up the receiver.

"Wade Kendell?" A man's voice. "I'm Kevin Garsten, AA&E Security."

"Yes, that's me," Kendell answered, still a little woozy from the sleep and the travel.

"Good that you made it in. Can you meet me in the bar downstairs?"

"Ten minutes okay?" Kendell replied, before hanging up, splashing water over his face, and putting on clean trousers and a cotton shirt.

***

There were two American men sitting at a small table in the lobby bar. The younger one got up as Kendell approached. He was even taller and leaner than Kendell. "Kevin Garsten." They shook hands. "This is my boss, Will Posey, chief of security."

Posey remained seated as he shook hands with Kendell. He looked to be in his forties, dark skin with straight black hair, somewhat overweight, cigarette dangling from his lips. A can of Falstaff beer stood on the table in front of Garsten's seat, while Posey was drinking a bourbon on the rocks. Garsten beckoned a waiter and ordered two more for them, and a beer for Kendell.

They sat down, and Posey spoke up: "Welcome to AA&E. Yep, Alcoholic Americans and Expats." This was a favorite line of his, to break the ice before the inevitable minutes of small talk that followed when a new face landed in-country.

The waiter soon reappeared and put down two cold Falstaffs, placed another bourbon on the table, and took away the empties. It occurred to Kendell that the staff here was very familiar with Garsten and Posey.

"Okay," said Posey, getting down to business. "Kevin here is about to hop on the bus around the corner. He's on night shift; starts at seven. The depot is at Ho Nai, thirty miles north of here, straight up Highway 1. You'll be on day shift, and you'll get the same bus at six in the morning, but not tomorrow. We'll send a driver at eight to take you to our Saigon office for processing, and to get you a

Department of Defense ID card. You'll need it for the PX and military clubs. Make sure you bring your passport. You'll be starting work the next day, so be on time for the bus then."

Garsten took over: "Don't change your dollars anywhere except with the Indian tailor shops around here. They'll give you the best rates. It's all illegal, but nobody gives a shit. If you want to drink, do it in this area. There's Mimi's bar around the corner, and near that is the Palace, which is fuckin' great and has better-looking girls. There's also Hai Ba Trung Street, and that's wall-to-wall bars. The ladies all drink Saigon tea, which is colored water. Some will drink a beer, but that'll cost you double. Gotta be careful, or you'll be spending big bucks. No girls are allowed in the hotels, but lots of these honeys have places nearby where they'll take guys for boom-boom."

Posey added, "I'd strongly advise you use protection if you're going to get laid. There's lots of clap and it's no fun unless you like the sensation of napalm fire coming out of your dick when you piss."

Garsten and Posey remained quiet as they finished their drinks, and then Garsten stood. "Well, I'm out of here. Welcome to Saigon."

Posey also got up. "Yeah. Me, too. Gotta make some rounds. You keep out of trouble and, oh, watch out for pickpockets … they're everywhere."

As they were leaving, Kendell thought that these guys were off-the-rail nuts … maybe had been in the war zone too long. However, as he craved another beer, he decided to check out one or two of Kevin's recommendations.

Chapter 4

First Look Around

It was a short walk to Mimi's around the corner. Kendell had to side-step some elderly street vendors squatting on the sidewalk, selling tropical fruits that he'd never seen before.

A rush of cool air hit him as the doorman opened up for him, and he stepped inside. Man, this is more like it, he thought. They had a good sound system, blasting out "You Really Got Me" by The Kinks, one of his favorites. The bar counter was on the left, and there was a line-up of foreign men, many in white shirtsleeves, others in safari suits, some seated, some standing, all drinking, smoking, talking. In and amongst them were attractive Vietnamese girls, most of them wearing revealing western clothes. The music and conversation and laughter all blended into one raucous melody. Kendell didn't like the thick cigarette smoke but, under the circumstances, was happy to tolerate it.

As the bar counter was full, Kendell turned to the other side of the place, which was set up with low tables and lounge sofas.

Numerous couples were sitting there; all foreign men with Vietnamese ladies. Kendell thought this must be where the Saigon teas happen. He was right.

"Hello. You like drink?" said a beautiful Vietnamese girl in a short skirt, hair hanging well below her slim waist.

"Give me an American beer," Kendell replied. He didn't care which kind. She spoke in Vietnamese to a waiter, who set off to the bar. Then she motioned for Kendell to take a seat with her, and cozied up beside him. She smelled great. The waiter was back in a flash with a tray, a can of ice-cold Hamm's beer, and a chilled glass.

"You like buy lady drink?" asked the waiter.

"Yeah, okay, maybe one," said Kendell.

"My name Mai. What's your name?" she said.

"Kendell. This is a nice bar. How long have you worked here?"

"I work here six month. I go school daytime. How long you been Vietnam?"

"Today is my first day."

A red Saigon tea arrived, and Kendell was surprised that she made it last as long as his beer, so he ordered another round. Her English was pretty good, he thought, as they asked questions of each other, with Mai asking most of them. He told her he was staying at the Catinat Hotel, was due to start work in Ho Nai, and would be looking for accommodation. She listened intently.

Kendell was loosening up after three beers, and asked Mai if she'd like to go out somewhere. She knew what he meant, and said, "I cannot because I don't know you well. But I have day off soon and, if you like, I take you to ABC club. Very good rock music there, and very cheap too. I off on Friday."

"Alright, sounds good to me. You meet me downstairs at the Catinat at 8:30 on Friday night, and we can go from there." He then motioned for the bill, which was 1,200 piastres; just six US dollars.

As he stood, she got up and hugged him. Her breasts felt wonderful pressed up against his lower chest. She said, "Okay, see you Friday night. I no forget."

It was still early. The next bar was the Palace, close to Mimi's, like Kevin Garsten had said. It was more of the same, but much bigger. When he entered, The Animals' "We've Gotta Get Out of this Place" was driving the beat. The place was rowdier than Mimi's, which Kendell didn't mind at all. He decided to sit at the well-stocked bar, and ordered another Hamm's, then turned and gazed at some of the girls sitting on the sofas. Almost all of them were smiling and looking his way. One of them caught his eye … mini skirt with tan legs, wearing a sleeveless blouse with plunging neckline. Her face was cute and her hair was done in a pixie cut, which suited her. He smiled back and she came right over to him and put her arm around his waist.

"My name Phung. What you name?"

"Kendell," he replied.

When she asked, he ordered a Saigon tea, and they sat and chatted about the same things he had with Mai. She seemed to be good company, and he bought another round. Man, the beers were kind of getting to him on an empty stomach, and this girl gulped her tea down rapidly. He decided to make his move. "Do you want to go out somewhere with me? You know some place?"

"Ya, I know good place, but you need to pay bar one thousand P because I finish early, and you also give me two thousand."

Kendell did the math…. This all added up to fifteen bucks. He could handle it, but with the cost of drinks thrown in, he'd have to be careful with his spending.

They squeezed into the back of a tiny blue and cream colored Renault taxi, the smallest car he had ever seen. He had to draw up his knees and bend his head down a bit to fit in. Phung gave instructions, and the driver pulled up to a closed shop two blocks away. Kendell paid him 100 piastres.

Phung rang a doorbell and an elderly lady opened the door. Phung then showed Kendell to a stairway and they went up one flight. She had a key for the room, and they went in and she turned on the light. The room was simple, clean, with a ceiling fan and attached bathroom. There was a door to a balcony facing the street.

"Okay, honey, I shower then you shower," said Phung as she disappeared into the bathroom.

Kendell stripped to his shorts and laid back on the bed, and a few minutes later she came out with a towel wrapped around her. When he tried to hug her, she said, "No, no. You shower first."

Reluctantly, Kendell took a cold shower, which didn't dampen his enthusiasm at all. He came back out to the bedroom with a towel around his waist. Phung had removed hers, and stood there looking like a goddess to him. Her breasts were amazing and her skin flawless. She seemingly didn't have body hair, and he doubted if she'd shaved it. He stepped up to her and she flicked off his towel, grabbed hold of his manhood, and led him to the bed.

***

An hour had gone by and Phung had slowly worn him down. He was sweating profusely, as the fan wasn't enough to cool him off. He took another cold shower, this time with Phung.

When they got dressed, she didn't ask, but Kendell handed her 2,000 piastres before they went down.

"How about money for taxi? It five hundred P."

He handed her a 500 note, and she hailed a pedicab. They both squeezed in, and the driver pedaled them back to the Catinat, where Kendell got out and she waved goodbye and carried on back to her home, or the Palace … Kendell wasn't sure.

He stood near the hotel entrance. All the excitement of the long trip and events of the day were suddenly weighing down on him. He was exhausted and hungry. It was close to 11:00 p.m. A foreign man was standing at a street vendor nearby, eating what looked like a baguette sandwich. Kendell asked him, "Is that good?" The guy nodded, so Kendell ordered one for 100 piastres and ate it right there. Whatever it was, it tasted delicious. He then went up to his room and was sound asleep well before midnight.

Chapter 5

Getting Organized

Kendell was an early riser. At 6:00 a.m. he got up, showered, dressed, and went downstairs for his complimentary buffet breakfast at the hotel café. There were many foreign men already sitting at the tables, and some looked very hungover. He thought he'd seen at least a few of them at Mimi's the night before. Kendell felt fine. He ordered scrambled eggs and ham, but couldn't drink the bitter Vietnamese coffee. He went back to his room at 7:00 and brushed his teeth. He looked out of his window … the day was seeing its first light.

At 8:00, the driver showed up at the entrance, and it was Minh. "Good morning Mr. Kendell, I take you main office. Nice to see you."

They drove off in what Kendell thought was the direction of the airport, but Minh took a different road than the one they'd been on the day before. This part of Saigon was working class, and very densely populated. There were sand-bagged security posts on the street corners, surrounded by concertina wire.

Here and there were bullet-ridden, rocket-blasted buildings, the results of the North Vietnamese Tet Offensive in the city, just a month earlier.

The AA&E office was on Plantation Road, lined with acacia trees, around the back side of Tan Son Nhat Air Base. Kendell spotted some damaged hangars and destroyed aircraft in the distance on the right side of the road. Along the left side was a lush golf course, with players making the rounds on the verdant fairways. The golf scene hardly resembled a war zone.

Minh parked outside the main office, and Kendell showed his passport to a guard and went in. At the reception desk, a pleasant, mature Vietnamese lady gave him a badge with his name on it, to be pinned to his shirt. She pointed him to the Admin department, second door on the left. There, a clerk directed him to sit and have his photo taken for a DOD identification card.

The next stop was Finance. A young lady in a light-green *áo dài* handed Kendell a form to fill out, on how he wanted to be paid. He'd come prepared, and entered the number and details of his joint bank account in California. He decided to have the company send Clara 1,000 dollars monthly, by bank transfer. The remaining 800 would be paid to him by company check. The lady then said, "Mr. Kendell, we pay at end of each month. Your American account will receive transfer one or two days after that, and your check for local expense will be given to you at Area 208. Now you can go outside to our canteen and someone will meet you there."

In the canteen, he ordered a Coke and took it to a small table, where he sat and surveyed the scene. There were two American soldiers at another table, in field uniforms, neither of them looking much older than teenagers. He then noticed a tall, light black American, standing, wearing a white, short-sleeved shirt that fit snugly against his obviously fit physique. He was speaking Vietnamese to the girl at the cash register. The guy soon noticed Kendell, and strolled up to him. "Hi. I'm Todd Carroll. I can see from your tag … you're Wade. Mind if I sit down?"

"Yeah, sure," said Kendell as they shook hands. "How are you doing?"

"Doing okay," Todd replied. "I normally work security out at Area 208, but I'm filling in here for a few days. I was in the Air Force, right here at Tan Son Nhat, before AA&E. Anyway, Will Posey asked me to get with you, to see if you need anything."

"Well, I've had my ID mugshot taken, and got my banking details squared away."

"Good. You're about finished here, then, but you can keep the driver for the rest of the day, to look around, see some rental apartments, whatever."

"That would be great," said Kendell. "Do you know of any good accommodation for rent?"

"We've got a weekly company newsletter. There are listings for apartments and villas. Most of us rent apartments. They run about a hundred fifty to two hundred fifty bucks per month, furnished. Some guys rent houses out in Thu Duc. It's closer to 208, but there isn't much else out there. You can grab a copy at reception."

"I'll do that," Kendell replied. "How about the defense ID card. They took the photo, but didn't give me anything?"

"Ah, they'll print that up and send it out to you at work," said Todd. "So, if you're all set, I'll probably see you out at 208. I've got to go check out a little fender-bender one of our expert drivers got involved in down the road here."

They both stood, shook hands again, and Todd strolled off.

Cool character, thought Kendell. He finished his Coke, went back to the reception lobby and took one of the newsletters, and turned in his badge. On his way out, he passed by Will Posey, who didn't notice or acknowledge him.

Back at the car, Kendell showed the apartment listings to Minh. "Can you bring me to see some of these?"

Minh scanned the page and then, pointing to one ad, said, "Yes I can do. This one on Tran Quy Cap Street. Many American live there."

They slipped back into the hectic traffic and drove to the first of the apartment listings. As it was in most of Saigon, the streets were lined with shophouses that had well-kept, colorful balconies on the upper levels, with potted flowers, plants, and balustrades of many designs. Most were four or five stories; the upper floors were apartments, with the ground floors being used for retail business. They pulled up in front of one of these, at 151 Tran Quy Cap.

Minh had a word with an elderly gentleman who was the landlord. He slowly led them upstairs to the third-floor apartment. It had two small bedrooms with ceiling fans, and a living room with simple furniture. The open-air kitchen was separated from the apartment by the stairwell. A toilet and shower was right next to it. Kendell tried the faucets … there was little water pressure. He disliked everything about this apartment. He could smell the neighbor's cooking odors, the street noise was penetrating, and there was no elevator.

Minh took Kendell to two more apartments in the same vicinity. One of them was quite nice, but it was on the fourth floor, again with no elevator.

"Minh, yesterday you said you know where to rent a villa. Can we get some lunch downtown, then you take me to see one?"

***

Highway 1 ran north from the city. It started in Dakao suburb and soon crossed the Saigon River on the big suspension bridge that had recently been reopened after repairs to bomb damage. From the height of the bridge, Kendell could see many cargo ships lined up at Newport docks. Offloading war supplies was a round-the-clock operation. This was also where AA&E's engineering materials were loaded on trucks and transported to Area 208, thirty miles away.

Once they had crossed the bridge, things really got lively on the two-lane highway. American and South Vietnamese military trucks ruled the road. They were in a hurry, and the American drivers, in particular, pushed the pace, with air horns blasting. Motorcycles kept to the side, knowing that these big rigs would squash them and keep rolling if they got in the way. The view off the highway was in contrast to the madness on the road. It was all serene paddy fields, tall coconut groves, and fruit trees. Kendell saw his first water buffalo.

Thu Duc was just a dozen miles up the road. The residential village was on the west side of the highway. Minh pulled the Datsun up to a security gate and spoke with the guard, who handed him some keys and let them through. Kendell was liking what he was seeing. There were wide avenues, plenty of acacia and poinciana shade trees. The villas weren't close to each other, but rather secluded. Minh turned left at the second street. There were vacant building lots and a few villas. They stopped at the second one on the right.

"My old boss owner this villa. He live here before," said Minh.

It was of French colonial design, but not that old. Just single story, white with a dark-green tiled roof, built up on three-foot columns so that air could circulate under the house. There were tall windows with hinged shutters, which could be closed at night. It had a garden around it, with mango, palm, and more flowering red poincianas. There was a fine gravel driveway that could be swept clean of leaves and debris. The place had a charm to it.

Minh unlocked the tall, green double doors and showed Kendell in. There was an expansive living and dining area with nice, modern-looking teak furniture. It had a cathedral ceiling with three fans hanging from long shafts. There was a telephone on a side table. The master bedroom had its own bathroom. The bed was a good one, and there were built-in closets. The other two bedrooms were furnished, and shared a bathroom. The kitchen was western in style, and had a big Westinghouse refrigerator. Kendell tried the faucet and there was good water pressure. He could hear the pump kicking in.

"How much per month?" asked Kendell.

"He want three hundred American dollar every month. Free electric and water," replied Minh.

Kendell thought that this was a bit more than he had budgeted for, but he'd probably save money by not living downtown where all the nightlife was. "Okay, tell your old boss I'll give him two hundred seventy-five dollars a month, and if anything breaks in the house, I'm good at fixing it. But I can't move in until the first of next month, so I'll give twenty dollars key money if he'll hold it for me."

On the drive back to Saigon, they passed the wreckage of two cargo trucks, in separate areas. These were, in fact, contracted trucks that hauled materials to and from Area 208. Both cabs were mangled, and one was on its side in a paddy field. It looked like they had been pushed aside and left there, so as to clear the road. Kendell thought that it wouldn't have been a good ending for the drivers.

At the hotel, Kendell thanked Minh and released him. It was just 4:00 p.m. He went up, had a cool shower, and put on clean clothes. He sat in a big armchair, looking out at the balcony, thinking that his first two days in Saigon had added a little excitement into his life. So far, it wasn't dull, like his life in Lancaster. He'd be working in a supervisory position at 208, and hoped he could handle it. He had apprehension because he'd never had people working under him before.

He knew that he should set up an overseas call to Clara, but didn't feel like it. Kendell admitted to himself that he was relieved to be away from her and his routine back there. He sort of missed the kids, but figured they'd have a much better life from what he could provide by working here. He thought that this job might even be good for his marriage, which had been faltering. Clara was a good mother to the kids, but he hadn't gotten on well with her for a few years. Kendell wasn't a talker, and had a reticent way about him. In contrast, Clara was always chattering on, and didn't hold back on complaining. This was very annoying to him, as was her huge weight gain since having the children. She'd become obese, and he was disgusted by it. All in all, he knew that his situation was a classic case of having been too young and foolish to get married.

Kendell didn't want to think about California anymore. He was up for a cold beer, but he also knew that he'd have to wake up early to catch the bus. He wondered if Phung was at the Palace yet. If not, plan B was Hai Ba Trung Street.

In the end, plan B proved unnecessary. She was indeed there.

Chapter 6

Warm Welcome at Work

Shortly before six next morning, the bus driver checked off Kendell's name and let him board. Kendell took a window seat and sat there while more foreigners and Vietnamese office staff got on. He hoped that no one would sit next to him, but it wasn't to be. A young, tanned American with long hair, in a khaki shirt, took the seat beside him, and nodded to Kendell before closing his eyes. The bus roared to life and they were off to Ho Nai.

As they passed Thu Duc, Kendell's seat mate woke up. He looked around and said, "Oh, we're about halfway there. I'm Jay Chastain. Redwood City, California." He had a big white smile, and offered his hand to Kendell.

"Yeah, I'm from Lancaster, myself," offered Kendell. They conversed back and forth a bit, with Jay doing most of the talking. He told Kendell that he'd been with the Marines up in Quang Tri. He'd worked in logistics there, and was wounded in a rocket attack. Upon discharge, he'd put up with public hostility and scorn directed at veterans, back in the San Francisco area. He now intended to work and stay out of the US as long as possible.

Sunrise in Vietnam was at about 7:00 a.m. in March, so it was still dark. As they got closer to Area 208, Kendell and Jay looked straight ahead, through the bus windshield, and saw a brilliant orange glow on the horizon. However, what they were seeing wasn't sunrise … it was a big fire. It got bigger and higher as they closed the distance. Jay became excited. "Jesus Christ! I think the depot's on fire! These fuckers tried to burn it down last year, but we took control of it. I take care of the bridge timber yard, and we've found incendiary devices there before. Man, this looks a lot worse than the last one."

The bus pulled into a wide, gravel parking lot outside the Area 208 gate. A security guard told all the passengers to wait near the vehicle. The parking spot was on a slight rise overlooking the expanse of open storage, at a safe distance from the chaos. Staring out over it, Kendell was in awe. It was a huge inferno, with a constant deafening roar. Most of the depot was burning, spewing flames more than 150 feet into the air. Dense black smoke was being carried away from them by the wind.

There were frequent fiery explosions, with thunderous booms, which caused debris to fly in every direction.

Red fire trucks from nearby Long Binh and Bien Hoa bases were already in the yards, getting as close as they could to the blaze, unleashing volumes of water. This didn't seem to be having much effect. Two bulldozers were offloaded from big Army low-bed trucks. Mobile cranes and rough-terrain forklifts were being sent into the fray. There were ambulances, with lights flashing, on standby, and a large helicopter was circling all this mayhem, making even more noise and causing the black smoke to swirl.

Kendell and the others stood beside the bus watching the spectacular event for more than an hour when a tall, older man with a noticeably hunched back walked up and called out, "Where's Wade Kendell?"

Kendell raised his hand and the man approached. "Bob Keller. I run the equipment motor pool. C'mon, let's head over there. It's safe enough; the wind's blowing the other way."

The motor pool was a busy place. It was a series of tall, metal-roofed, open work bays for maintaining the trucks and heavy equipment. The plywood-and-tin admin block was attached at one end, and contained separate offices for the supervisors. Fortunately, each space had windows and was air-conditioned.

"I won't bullshit you … this place is in a mess," Keller said. "The depot's shut down until this fire is put out. We're only going to be fixing essential stuff until then. Don't worry if it looks like it's too much for you; it's not. These old Vietnamese mechanics know their shit. You just need to make sure they get their parts and you get your reports and paperwork in on time. You'll meet Ralph Gates, and he'll school you on all this. It's simple. This ain't a high-tech contract. AA&E would hire a warm body to fill any position if they could make a buck. The Army loves paperwork, so they know what's going on and who to hang it on if things go wrong."

Keller led the way into Kendell's new office, which housed not much more than a desk and chair, and a notice board behind it with the names of all his mechanics. They talked for a while about some of the general routines, and then Keller went off to do his own work.

In the meantime, Kendell busied himself scanning through some vehicle technical manuals that were lying on the desk, while every now and then wandering outside to observe the conflagration.

***

Mid-morning, Ralph Gates came into the office and introduced himself to Kendell. He was short, looked fit, with neat, wavy black hair and reddish cheeks. It turned out that he was an ex-special forces combat medic. He returned to work in Vietnam shortly after he completed his service, and had married a Vietnamese woman in Saigon.

"I got word that the fire has reached the asphalt yard," he said. "It's stacked six high with fifty-gallon drums, and there are acres of it. The drums explode, the asphalt thins with the heat, then runs into the ditches and spreads fire everywhere. Can't put it out with water. It's got to the oxygen and acetylene pressure containers, which are popping off and rocketing sky high. The Army engineers have decided to just contain it, let it burn itself out."

Ralph showed Kendell the blank forms he would need to fill out for parts requests and daily job reporting, and ran him through some of the other routines at the motor pool. The day was now staggeringly hot, with the added heat radiating from the massive fire. Because of that, and the slow work roster as a result of the blaze, Ralph said they should go to lunch early. "We'll take the jeep over to the 199th. The enlisted men's club. It's not far. They've got good burgers, steaks, and cold beer. Some super looking waitresses, especially the Cambodian chick."

The 199th Light Infantry Brigade Club was air-conditioned, and Ralph was right about the Cambodian girl ... she was a knockout. Kendell enjoyed the long lunch, and felt like he wanted to spend rest of the day there but, instead, they got back on the dusty road and returned to 208. It seemed that the fire had gained in intensity. Two female laborers were being given oxygen, by medics, next to an ambulance, after the fumes had gotten to them in the yard.

The remainder of the day passed slowly, as there wasn't much to do except wander in and out of the office to observe the fire. As the bus pulled up at 6:45 with the night crew, the day shift was already waiting. Kevin Garsten stepped off and noticed Kendell. "Hey, looks like I'm late for the barbecue. Any hot dogs left?"

It was getting dark. The huge blaze looked even more fear-provoking than it had in the morning. Kendell closed his eyes and slept the entire way back to Saigon.

Chapter 7

Saigon Streets

Kendell very soon got into a routine of sorts. He decided to stay at the hotel for the full two weeks afforded by the company. He was comfortable there, could sign for his meals, and there were a lot of good bars nearby.

Each morning, when he arrived at Area 208, he noticed there was less intensity to the fire. By the fifth day, it had just about burned out, and there remained just smoldering pockets of it. Bulldozers were at work pushing all the burnt debris and rubble into a ravine that ran along the southern perimeter of the depot. Graders were resurfacing the gravel roads. At least ten trucks arrived each hour in the yards to begin replacing the materials that had been destroyed in the blaze.

Things quickly got back to normal at the motor pool. Kendell felt that his new job was going well. Like Bob Keller had said … the place pretty much ran by itself.

He managed to call Clara from the operations office. He told her that things were going well, but didn't mention the fire. She told him the children were fine, then went on to complain about having to wait until the end of the month for the money transfers. After that conversation, Kendell decided he'd be calling her just once every month.

He was enjoying his evenings in Saigon. By 8:30 p.m. he'd be showered and ready to bar hop for two or three hours. He'd already checked out the bars on Hai Ba Trung Street. Most of them were a bit stale, but a lot cheaper than Tu Do Street. American GIs took to these bars, and the girls there took to them. Little Renault taxis were standing by, outside, to take these lovebirds to and from their nests. The Ritz was the best bar on Hai Ba Trung, Kendell thought. It was a bit classy compared to others like the Tennessee. The girls there all wore the *áo dài*, which he found alluring. He thought that, before long, he'd have to ask one of these ladies for a live demonstration on how to remove one. He envisioned his big wife wearing one, which made him shake his head and think about something else.

***

On the Friday night of his first week, after showering and changing clothes, he went down to the hotel lobby. It was 8:30, and there she was, just as she'd promised. It was

Mai, from Mimi's, and Kendell thought that she was gorgeous, wearing her tight fitting, hip-cut jeans with a white, sleeveless, cotton blouse, and long glossy black hair cascading off her shoulders. She looked so fresh and uncomplicated. She didn't even carry a purse.

"Are you ready to go to ABC club? We can walk there," she said. They left the hotel and she walked close to him. He took her hand and she gently squeezed his.

They walked straight down to the end of Tu Do Street and turned left at the Saigon River frontage road. The far bank was undeveloped, and in the distant countryside one could see parachute flares drifting slowly down. Helicopters were busy delivering streams of bright-red tracer bullets and rockets to their targets. Whenever the traffic noise subsided, the faint sounds of chopper rotors, gunfire, and explosions could be heard. Kendell thought, it's good to be on this side of the river. They continued strolling along the river drive, where there were scattered groups of refugees from the war zones, already stretched out for the night and sleeping on the bare sidewalk.

They then came up to a traffic circle and turned to the left. Along the crescent he saw the place, a single-story building with a large, illuminated sign, "ABC Bar," glowing above the entrance door. Shops to the left and right of it were closed for the night, but hundreds of motorcycles were parked along the roadside.

The solid beat of music could be heard and felt as Kendell paid the cover charge of 120 piastres each, to the door girl. There was no security check, just a sign at the entrance, in Vietnamese and English: "No firearms allowed."

Inside, it was almost deafening. There were rows of tiered seats, each having a view of the stage. A waitress showed them to an upper row. Kendell had to shout his order to her. "Two Hamm beers." Between the seats and stage was a large dance floor, full of foreign men and Vietnamese girls, locked to each other, slow-dancing to "Time Is On My Side." The ABC band was doing an excellent job on the Rolling Stones' hit song.

The waitress brought the drinks and placed them on a narrow shelf between their seats, along with a plastic cup that contained the tab. It had become a bit louder, as the band got into The Who's "I Can See For Miles."

Mai leaned into Kendell and spoke loudly over the music, into his ear, "This is best band in Vietnam. They all same family, brothers and sisters. Before they so poor, but play good music and Americans like them very much." As she said this, she got so close to him that her lips touched his ear several times, and he felt her warm breath. He was loving every moment of it. She added, "Thank you for take me out tonight, I very happy come here with you." He turned to face her and she kissed him firmly on his lips for a full minute. Kendell was awed.

The youngest and smallest ABC band member, a diminutive teenager, had a powerful singing voice, and she was the crowd favorite. They gave her thunderous applause after each song. What a great bar, thought Kendell. He and Mai could smell the odor of marijuana above the cigarette smoke in the bar, and they thought nothing of it.

After two beers, Kendell ordered another, but Mai switched to Coca-Cola. As the waitress came back with their drinks on a tray, there was a huge, blinding bright flash, and a deafening explosive crack, followed by immediate darkness and silence. The force of the blast had thrown the waitress into Kendell. He was stunned and confused but, in a moment, realized that a bomb had exploded near the stage. The waitress was draped over him and his seat. He grasped her by the waist and rolled her to his left side, then began feeling around for Mai on his right. He could feel her legs; her upper body was wedged between two seatbacks. Her hand found his, and he pulled her towards him. They hugged each other in silence.

The darkness ended with the ignition of smoldering debris near the stage. As it began to burn, it was possible for Kendell to see the damage. The entire roof was hanging, and looked about to collapse. Stunned people were standing, but others were prone and strewn about. Wreckage was everywhere. The flames were increasing and he could now see Mai. "Are you okay?" he weakly whispered, and she nodded. He saw the waitress, who was now sitting on the floor beside him, dazed. He knew that they had to get out of there quickly. He lifted Mai to her feet, and helped the waitress to stand. He held both of them by their arms.

There were men at the entrance, with flashlights shining, so Kendell headed towards them with the two girls. Others were following, shifting debris out of their way as they escaped. When they reached the sidewalk, police were already arriving on the scene, along with fire and rescue services. As survivors were streaming out of the club, firemen were going in, dragging water hoses. Medics were bringing stretchers in to carry the casualties.

Kendell led Mai a short distance away, where they stopped under a tree and examined themselves. They didn't seem to have any injuries, but both were in shock and somewhat confused. They gazed back towards the ABC and could now see flames leaping up from the broken roof. The ringing in Kendell's ears was lessening, and he was able to talk. "Let's go. Are you okay to walk?"

She shook her head. "No, we get cyclo. I go to Mimi's. Mamasan will take care me. You go back to hotel, get sleep. You have to work morning."

They found a cyclo and had the driver pedal them over to Mimi's. It was empty. Police had immediately cleared all the bars following the explosion.

"Goodnight, and don't worry. I'll see you tomorrow," Kendell said to Mai as he hugged her and then turned to walk back to his hotel.

***

The next morning, Kendell slept on the bus to Area 208. He was calming down from the wild events of the previous night, but was kind of glad to find Todd Carroll in the operations office.

"Hey, Kendell. Good to see you again. Everything okay?"

"Alright, I guess, but I need to tell you something. Last night, I was in the ABC bar, down by the river, and the place got fucking blown up while I was there!"

"Yeah, I already got the brief on this one," Todd replied. "Are you sure you're alright … no injuries?"

Kendell nodded. "Somehow I'm okay. I got out of there and immediately left the area…. Do I need to report this, or what?"

"As long as you're sure you're not hurt, I'll pretend you didn't tell me. We've got too many other security issues going on, especially since the depot got sabotaged. Any problem with that?"

"No problem at all," Kendell said. "I should tell you that I was also with a lady, but she's okay, too."

Todd sighed. "I didn't hear that, either."

"Shit, I don't really know what happened to any of the other people."

"One GI and one girl were killed outright," Todd told him. "Looks like the bomb didn't have a lot of shrapnel in it. The girl singer got struck in the leg, but she'll survive. Some are hospitalized, but I don't have any details on their conditions."

Before he turned to leave, Todd added, "If you're going to be out catting around in the evenings, best to keep away from the crowds. The ABC was just too tempting a target. Go to the smaller bars. They never get blown up."

***

That night, Kendell didn't want to leave the hotel, but he made a short visit to Mimi's to check on Mai. She saw him as he walked in, and immediately rushed up to embrace him. She was sobbing. "Oh, Kendell, I'm so sorry I take you to ABC. I can't believe what happened! I feel so bad."

They sat down in the lounge area. After a while, she calmed down, and Kendell said, "Never mind, we're both okay, but I was worried about you all day. Maybe you need some rest tonight, same as me. I'll pay the bar and you can go home early and sleep."

She was genuinely touched by this, and leaned over to kiss him. "Oh, thank you. No need to buy drinks tonight. You go back to hotel and sleep now." She hugged him and kissed him again. "I going to miss you until I see you again."

Kendell had trouble getting to sleep. He'd been in-country just one week, and so much had happened. He thought it over. Never in his life had he experienced excitement like this. He knew that he was being exposed to danger, and there was violence everywhere in the country, but he didn't even consider going back to California. He felt alive here.

He finally drifted off to sleep, thinking of Mai.

***

There was more tragedy the next morning, when Kendell witnessed an accident on the way to 208. A two-and-a-half-ton truck going in the opposite direction drifted off to the shoulder and slammed an old man wearing a straw hat, pushing a bicycle laden with his wares. The man and his goods were sent flying as the truck blasted its horn and powered on. The man landed hard, some distance away. Kendell had been gazing out at the paddy fields on that side of the bus, and saw it all. Jesus, the fucking driver just kept going!

That evening, Kendell saw that the body was still right where it had landed. The goods were scattered and picked over, but the man remained where he had died. His straw hat was gone.

Kendell drank a lot that night. He hit the Tennessee bar first. It was noisy, smoke-filled, and rowdy with GIs letting off steam. He didn't buy any Saigon teas, but spotted Jay Chastain, who shouted above the clamor, "Hey, Kendell. This place is crazy tonight! You want a drink?"

Kendell replied, "Fuck yeah, thanks. But it probably won't be enough."

They fell into conversation about recent events, and then Kendell changed the topic: "Say, do you know anyone who likes to play poker?"

"You're looking at him," Jay replied. "I love a good game of five card draw once in a while."

"Me, too. I think I'll be renting a villa pretty soon, and I'd like to get a weekly game going. You know any other guys who play?"

"Sure, there's plenty of guys up for that. Let me know when you get set up. Hey, after this, let's hit the Ritz. Too fuckin' many drunk GIs in here, and there's bound to be a fight."

The Ritz was busy as well, but most of the customers were civilian contractors and news correspondents. Jay said, "I really dig this place. It's a little pricey, but it's good bang for the buck, and I mean that literally. Love these Vietnamese dresses."

Kendell bought Jay a beer and motioned for one of the girls to come to the bar. She was tall, with a small waist and ample breasts, accentuated by the lines of the *áo dài*, which all of the hostesses wore here. She said her name was "Thuy," and it sounded like "Twee" to Kendell. She had a pretty, Chinese look to her. He told her his name and ordered her a Saigon tea.

Jay invited a shorter girl over, and he and Kendell continued putting down the Hamm's, one can after another. There was a good sound system, playing a lot of Creedence and Steppenwolf. Later, Jay leaned to Kendell and half-shouted, "I just asked this sweetie if she wants to see my stamp collection at my place, so we're getting out of here. Anyway, it costs too goddam much here, so we're rolling. See you tomorrow."

Kendell stayed and drank more and was losing control. "Miss Twee, do you have a room somewhere? I want you to show me how to take off that beautiful dress."

Thuy said, "Okay, I show you, but you have to pay bar and I cannot stay all night."

At her room, Kendell got the education he was looking for. Just a few snap buttons to pop, then pull the arms out of the sleeves, and the top is off. Next was the bottom part; silky trousers with an elastic waistband, which took just a second to remove. What a great design. She stood there in a white strapless bra and bikini panties. These came off even quicker than the *áo dài*. She was skinny, but had big, firm breasts. Drunk, Kendell still couldn't help but think of Mai. He missed her, so he said to Thuy, "Thank you for the show. I'll see you another time." He handed her 2,000 piastres, which she seemed pleased with.

He was back at the hotel and in bed before midnight.

***

Earlier in the week, almost right after he had driven Kendell around to view the properties, Minh had left a message for Kendell at the hotel. It said that a Mr. Phuc had agreed to his offer of 275 dollars per month for the villa at Thu Duc, and wanted to meet Kendell on Thursday night at the hotel.

Kendell returned from work, showered, and waited for Mr. Phuc in the lobby. The man arrived on time. He was tall for a Vietnamese, slim build. His hair was trim, parted, and combed back. He wore a white, long-sleeved shirt, tucked neatly into his trousers. He appeared cultured and educated. "Very nice to meet you, sir. I'm Nguyen Van Phuc. Just call me Phuc." He pronounced it as "Fook." His English was perfect. Kendell introduced himself.

"Mr. Kendell, if you still wish to rent my villa, it's available for the price you have offered. It's a very good home. I had it built for my family, but my company required me to move to Danang. Two hundred, seventy-five dollars in advance, and you can move in."

Kendell said, "Yes, I want to rent it, but I can't pay until the end of this month."

"That will be fine. I have here a one-year contract. The payment must be in US dollars, but I can also accept your personal US-dollar check."

"Great," Kendell replied. "If you'll excuse me, I'll go up and get my checkbook, and we can do that right now."

Kendell returned to the lobby and they discussed some of the contract details. They both signed the document, and Kendell wrote the check, with the payee line left blank, as Phuc requested.

Phuc got up and said, "Thank you very much, Mr. Kendell. I'm very fond of Americans, and I know that you'll take care of the house. I'll make a copy of the contract for you, and have Minh deliver it to you with the keys. You've made a very good decision."

Right after the meeting, Kendell headed straight over to Mimi's. He felt excited about getting his own residence, and he wanted to see Mai. He ordered drinks and told her about the villa. "Are you going to visit me there?" he asked.

Mai answered, "For sure, but I don't know the way there, and maybe the security man not let me in."

"Don't worry about that. My driver Minh can take you there the first time. He can get you past security."

***

It was Mai's day off, and she'd told Kendell that she wanted to surprise him and take him somewhere different. That night, they met in the Catinat lobby and she led him out to the pedicab that had brought her there. They squeezed into the narrow seat and the driver, behind them, began pedaling. He wore a pith helmet, similar to what the Viet Cong guerrillas wore. The cyclo's folding roof had been lowered, as it was a clear night.

They meandered through the dense, slow-moving traffic, Kendell's arm around Mai's shoulders. The sidewalks were cluttered with pedestrians and vendors of all sorts, which was still fascinating to him, and he occasionally asked Mai what this or that strange food item was. It made for a picturesque, if chaotic, scene, as many of the streets were lined with tall, mature trees from the French colonial times, with trunks that soared straight up to a great height before branching out.

After a half hour or so, the cyclo stopped in front of a double-wide shophouse that was a Vietnamese restaurant named Pho 50, Nguyen Trai, taken from the name of the street. The front was open to the sidewalk, busy with street life. A few tables stood outside, under an awning. Mai took Kendell inside, where most of the customers were eating at tables beneath overhead fans. "You like try *pho* soup? It Vietnam noodles. Many people like it. You can have beef or chicken."

Kendell just nodded and said, "I'll try beef. Can I get a beer here?" He wasn't keen on noodles, but would try it, to be polite. Mai said something to a waiter and, in minutes, two bowls of *pho* were brought to their table, followed by a large bottle of Bière 33 with two glasses and a bucket of ice. Kendell noticed that other customers were drinking the 33 with ice, so he didn't object when the waiter put ice in their glasses and poured the beer over it. There was a plate on the table with fresh mint leaves and bean sprouts. Mai used chopsticks to add both to their bowls. There were clean spoons and forks in a cup. She handed Kendell one of each. Cut, red chili peppers and fish sauce were on the table, but he didn't want any of that.

Kendell found that the *pho* was actually really delicious, and somehow the iced beer went well with it. He was enjoying himself as much as he did in the bars, but in a different way. What a beautiful country this could be, if it weren't for the war. He looked at Mai with her serene smile and he felt happy.

She said, "I bring you here because I want you to see the place I live. It next door to here. Room rent to girls only. No men can stay. Sometime I eat here before go to work. My study class not far from here."

Mai paid the bill – 200 piastres, or about one dollar – and, before getting back into the cyclo, she pointed up to a balcony next door. "That my room," she said.

Kendell nodded and sighed, knowing that he couldn't go up there with her.

Chapter 8

Settling in at Thu Duc

Kendell had used up all of his time at the Catinat, and Ralph Gates had given him the day off, to move out to Thu Duc. At check-out time, Minh was waiting outside with the Datsun, along with a copy of the villa rental contract and the keys.

The doorman loaded Kendell's luggage into the trunk of the car, and Kendell tipped him 100 piastres. Then they were off to Thu Duc. Upon arrival, at the security gate, Minh had a discussion with the two old guards, who were both smoking. "I tell them that you stay here now. They say if you want anything, you tell them. It good to be friend with them."

Kendell looked around the villa, to see what he'd need to buy, but, surprisingly, it was very complete. There were clean pillows and sheets on the bed, and fresh towels in the closet. The kitchen had pots and pans, plates, glasses, cups, and cutlery. About all he needed was food for the cupboard, drinking water, bread, butter, coffee, sugar. By now he'd received his DOD ID card, which had been sent out to the depot, so he made a list and asked Minh to take him out to the post exchange.

With the ID card, Kendell now had access to all the US military PXs, commissaries, clubs, hospitals, and other facilities. At the 199th Post Exchange, he found everything he needed, plus three cases of Falstaff beer in cans, which was the limit allowed for one month.

All payments at the military outlets had to be in military payment certificates, or MPCs. These were paper notes with the dollar value printed on them; a brainchild of the Department of Defense. The GIs got their local pay in MPC, and the idea was to keep them from spending US dollars off base. Most of the Americans referred to MPCs as "funny money." Nobody wanted it, but it was bought and sold on the black market. Kendell bought his MPCs from one of the Indian tailors near the hotel. For 100 US dollars, he received 140 in MPCs. This made for huge discounts with his on-base spending.

After getting his supplies at the PX, Kendell was a bit hungry, and decided to go to the 199th for lunch. Minh wasn't allowed in, so he found a spot, shaded from the sun, and stood by with the car.

Inside the club, the air-conditioning felt good, and Kendell saw Ralph Gates already sitting with another guy at a table near the end of the bar.

"I thought you were moving today," said Gates.

"Yeah, I am, but I had to hit the PX and buy a bunch of stuff for the new place," Kendell replied. "Thought I'd stop by for lunch."

"Sit down," Ralph said. "This here's Tom Clarke, area supervisor of our depot operations." He then turned in his chair towards a tall, slim man in jeans and black T-shirt, who stood at the bar. "And this is Cal Cole, assistant area supervisor." Kendell shook hands with both of them.

"Ralph says you're out at Thu Duc," said Tom. "I almost rented a place there, but it's too damn quiet for me. I'd be running back and forth to Saigon, and that's not a good idea, especially at night."

Tom and Cal both had beers in front of them, while Ralph was drinking Coke. Kendell thought that Tom looked like a more handsome version of Duane Eddy. Both Tom and Cal had slicked-back, dark hair, wore western boots, and radiated a sort of rebellious confidence.

The Cambodian waitress came by to take their orders, and all four men decided on the same thing … deluxe hamburger with fries. Tom commented, "Cal's not sitting with us today. He prefers to stand. He's had a little accident."

"Oh, man, here we go again. You just can't leave it alone, can you?" said Cal.

Ignoring Cal's mild irritation, Tom added, "Yeah, he was coming down the final stretch to 208 on his Honda this morning, and on the last turn the bike hit some spilt oil and skidded out from under him. He went sliding down the road on his ass, and his Beretta went off in his back pocket. He shot himself in the ass. We all heard it, and saw him come limping up to the gate…. War is hell."

"Fuck no!" Cal responded "I didn't actually shoot myself in the ass. It's just powder burns…. But I'm gonna have to get that hole in my jeans pocket mended, as soon as I send 'em to the laundry and get the shit stains washed out."

When their raucous laughter subsided, the men conversed back and forth over lunch, and Tom and Cal said that they often went to Mimi's, although Kendell hadn't noticed either of them the few times he'd been there.

Tom said that he also owned a Honda 305 scrambler. He and Cal rode to and from work, and seldom took the bus. He told Kendell that, should he ever want to spend a night in Saigon, instead of going home to Thu Duc, he could put him on to a little hotel that wouldn't cost a lot and didn't have restrictions on guests. Kendell said, "Thanks, I might take you up on that."

***

That evening, at the villa by himself, Kendell realized that this was the quietest place he'd been since arriving in Vietnam. About the only sounds came from a few crickets and frogs outside, and the humming of the ceiling fans. He had no radio, TV, or recorded music. He wasn't much of a reader, but he had no books with him anyway.

The beers that he'd put into the freezer compartment were cold already, so he took one out, went through the tall front doors, sat on the tiled steps in the shadows, and popped it open. It tasted so refreshing after the long, hot day, and he soon went in to get another. The next few hours, he sat and drank, contemplating his new life, before retiring to bed.

In the morning, he had to walk a few minutes out to the highway, and on the bus into 208 he had some ideas about what might improve his evenings at Thu Duc. First of all, he needed some music, so when he got to the motor pool, he mentioned this to Ralph.

"You know what? You're in luck. We had a guy who worked here named Copeland. He quit and disappeared. His Panasonic reel-to-reel is still in his office. He used to play rock and roll on it and annoy everyone. You can take it for now, and if he don't show up again, you can have it. But I don't think he's coming back, because I heard he got dusted in Cambodia."

"That's a pity," Kendell replied, not really meaning it. "But thanks." He then paused for a moment before putting his next idea to Ralph. "Also, do you know where I can get a handgun … something like what Cal carries?"

"Easy. Cal knows a South Vietnamese Army captain who sells all kinds of small arms. I'll tell Cal you're interested."

That afternoon, Kendell wrote a note to Mai and invited her to the villa. In the message, he told her Minh could bring her there, and gave her Minh's number. On the bus back in the evening, he asked Jay Chastain to deliver the message to her at the bar.

Kendell had already called Minh and told him she might call. The next morning, Jay told Kendell that he'd seen Mai and she'd read the note, but she didn't send a reply.

***

Two days had gone by and Kendell hadn't heard from Mai, or Minh. He got down from the bus at Thu Duc and walked through the estate's security gate. The two guards were smiling and smoking, as usual, and one of them tried to tell Kendell something, but he still couldn't understand a word of Vietnamese. Nearing the villa, he saw the Datsun parked in the drive, and Minh standing beside it, talking with Mai, who was seated on the front steps.

She looked happy to see him, and gave him her serene smile, but without saying anything. Her long hair was pulled up into to a bun, which accentuated her cheekbones and made her look elegant. She wore a long-sleeved, plain white tunic without a collar, over black trousers. On her feet were flip-flop sandals. Her straw hat and a woven basket were by her side.

"Wow, big surprise!" said Kendell with a grin on his face.

Minh was already getting in the car and was preparing to drive off, but Kendell tried to delay him for a moment. "Thanks, Minh. Let me pay you for this."

"Never mind, Mr. Kendell. Enjoy evening." And he drove off without taking any money.

Kendell unlocked the front door and they went in. He switched on some lights and the overhead fans. Mai put down her hat and basket on the coffee table, and turned to face Kendell. They immediately embraced and practically fell onto the sofa, kissing passionately.

"Come on … you show me bedroom, and we shower," said Mai. She had left her sandals on the steps, and she now helped Kendell to unlace and remove his boots.

They went into the bedroom, hurriedly stripped to their underwear, and entered the bathroom, where the remaining garments came off. Kendell was stunned by the beauty of Mai's body. They showered together, and she soaped and rinsed him, not inhibited by their nakedness or by his obviously aroused condition.

They but half-dried themselves and tumbled on to the white sheet of the big bed. In the three weeks they had known and become fond of each other, a lot of sexual passion had been building, and now it was all coming out. There was nothing in their minds except the sensual pleasures they were experiencing. They reached fulfillment at nearly the same moment, then rolled onto their backs, beneath the slow ceiling fan. Mai kissed him and got up to shower again. When she returned, he had almost drifted off to sleep, and she had to rouse him and make him go for another shower.

He came back out of the bathroom and put on clean shorts, then found Mai in the kitchen. She was wearing Vietnamese pajamas, which she'd brought in her basket. She handed him a cold Falstaff, which was what he most wanted right then. She'd also brought some sausage baguettes, and handed Kendell one on a plate. He suddenly realized how famished he was, and enjoyed every bite of it. Mai ate some sticky rice and mango, which came wrapped in a banana leaf. She gave a bit to Kendell, and he liked it.

They finished the snacks and went into the living room, where Kendell started the Panasonic reel-to-reel. It had a lot of Motown music … Marvin Gaye, The Supremes, The Shirelles. He set the volume low, joined Mai on the comfortable sofa, and put his arm around her. She had nothing on beneath the pajamas, and he tried to unbutton her top with his free hand. With her own hands, she completed the task for him, and he went right to kissing her firm breasts. The Shirelles' hit "Will You Still Love Me Tomorrow" was first on the tape playlist, and within moments they had descended into the same passion that had overwhelmed them in the bedroom.

***

In the morning, they walked in the quiet shade of the acacia trees, out to the bustling main highway. Wearing her *nón lá*, Mai looked like the other Vietnamese ladies who were waiting for their local transport.

"Okay, I get bus here back to Saigon," she said. "Next time I come back by myself. No need to send driver. Take care, honey." She squeezed his hand and scrambled onto a beaten-up, top-heavy, overloaded bus, which roared off in a cloud of black diesel smoke and dust.

In a few minutes, the AA&E bus came along, and, for the first time, the company transport looked very comfortable to Kendell, compared to the public buses that rattled up and down the highway.

The day passed slowly until Cal Cole stopped by in the afternoon and asked

Kendell to come out to where he'd parked his jeep. He pulled out an olive-green Army toolbag from beneath the seat, and unzipped it to reveal several handguns. "Alright, there's a few of those little 25-caliber Berettas; two Colt 45 Army automatics; and one Smith & Wesson .38 Model 14. They're all twenty bucks apiece, and I can get lots of cheap ammo. What d'ya think?"

"I like the thirty-eight," said Kendell. "How much for the ammo?"

"Ten bucks will get you two hundred rounds. I can get it all to you tomorrow. Maybe stop by to see that house of yours after work?"

"It's a deal. See you then," said Kendell.

Later, he was having a bit of difficulty focusing on his job at the motor pool. There wasn't so much for him to do when things were running smoothly, and he kept thinking of Mai. Reluctantly, he made a call to Clara. It was about 5:00 p.m. in California. She sounded agitated when she picked up; said she'd had a busy and tiring day, and now she had to cook dinner for the kids. He asked about them and she said they were both fine. She didn't ask anything about him or his work. It was a brief conversation, and Kendell felt relieved when it ended.

***

Cal came to the villa as promised the next evening, on his Honda. Kendell heard him roaring up to a stop in front of the house, and went out to the porch to greet him.

Cal straddled the bike, revved the engine before turning it off, and said, "Hey man. Nice place…. I could use a cold beer."

"No problem. Come on in," replied Kendell. He got two cold Falstaffs out of the fridge and placed them on the dining table, where they both took seats.

This time, Cal had brought a smaller canvas bag with the .38 revolver that Kendell wanted. He placed it on the table with four small boxes of ammo. "It's all here … pistol and 200 rounds." He suggested that they take the gun out back of the house and test fire it.

Kendell wanted to, but said, "I think the security guards might not go for that."

"Those guys are next to the highway; probably won't hear it," Cal said. "And these houses aren't on top of each other … some of them even look vacant…. Let's give it a go."

Kendell nodded, so they put their drinks down and walked out behind the house. At the edge of the back lot was an acacia tree. There was a shallow ravine behind it, with steps going down, made up of sandbags. Kendell hoisted one of the heavy bags and placed it against the tree. They walked back to the rear of the house and Cal loaded the pistol with six rounds from his pocket, and handed it to Kendell.

"Alright … I hope this doesn't bring the guards down on us," said Kendell, before firing off one shot.

They walked up to the sandbag, and near the center of it was a bullet hole. So far, there was no commotion in the neighborhood.

"Nice shot," said Cal. "Do two more rounds, then let's give it five minutes … see if anyone has a problem."

Cal lit a cigarette as they went back, and Kendell fired two more shots from the same position.

They waited … Cal finished his smoke … but the guards didn't come, and none of the neighbors made any complaint.

Kendell handed the pistol to Cal, who fired the three remaining shots, after which they observed the six holes in the sandbag.

"Looks like you're good to go," said Cal as they walked back to the dining table and finished their beers.

Before Cal left, Kendell said they should soon get a card game going, to which Cal readily agreed, before starting up the Honda and blasting off in a trail of dust and gravel.

Kendell went back to the fridge and then turned on the reel-to-reel. He wanted Mai to be there. He didn't really know when she'd be back, if at all. He thought that if she didn't come by the weekend, he'd ride the company bus to Saigon after work, take a hotel, and look for her at Mimi's.

The remainder of the week was uneventful. He stocked up on canned food and snacks at the 199th PX, which only reminded him that his one good meal of the day would usually be at the club, with Ralph.

***

On Friday evening, he got off the bus at the highway, as usual, and walked past the security point into the Thu Duc estate. The sun was about to set, giving off a pleasant amber glow, which filtered through the trees. As he approached the villa, a gentle voice spoke out from the shade of some palms, "Hello Mr. Kendell, remember me?" In a second, he realized it was Mai. She was sitting on a little Honda motorbike, wearing jeans with a white blouse, and was clutching her *nón lá*. He was taken aback at first, then strode up to her smiling face. He put his arms around her and they kissed like lovers.

"Come on, let's go in," he said. She untied and removed a cloth bundle from her motorbike, and Kendell unlocked the front door. Inside, they resumed kissing and, without speaking, went straight to the bathroom to shower together. The water was warm from the day's heat on the tank tower. They kept kissing and embracing with the water cascading over them. Mai looked so alluring and exotic to Kendell, her body glimmering from the water and her long hair splashed over her smooth shoulders and breasts. They had barely toweled their bodies dry before crashing, entwined, on to the bed in a heated passion that was even more torrid than on their last encounter.

Later, they showered again, but not in such haste. Wade put on shorts, and Mai wore one of his T-shirts. She'd brought more items this time. As she opened her bundle, Kendell noted several changes of clothes. There was also uncooked rice, noodles, eggs, onions, garlic, fresh pork and chicken, fish sauce, and seasonings. She went to the kitchen and did up a pan of garlic fried pork with onions and steamed rice, which tasted so delicious to Kendell, compared to the canned food he'd mostly been eating. After dinner, they talked for a while and listened to the tapes, and went to sleep early. Kendell was very contented.

***

Kendell woke before the alarm, and heard birds singing in the garden. As he stirred, Mai opened her eyes and smiled at him, and soon they rolled their naked bodies together for an early, heated resumption of the previous night's activity.

For breakfast, Mai made scrambled eggs, fried noodles, and coffee, and Kendell was pleased when she told him she could stay the weekend.

"That's great. But what will you do today while I'm working?" he asked.

"I will just stay here, read my books, maybe go Thu Duc market to buy food. But I just get one day off, so another two days I must pay bar two thousand P."

"No problem, I got that," he told her.

As he sipped his coffee, he became more curious about something that had been at the back of his mind. He thought for a moment, then asked her how much she made per month at Mimi's, and she told him usually it was 50,000 to 60,000 piastres, which was between 230 and 270 dollars. She was exaggerating a bit, but not by much.

He kissed her and went out the door.

On the bus and at work all day, he thought about what she'd told him. It was so much better, being in the villa with her. Aside from the sexual intimacy, he enjoyed her company very much. Then, he thought, there was the security benefit of having someone at the house while he was at work. And he assumed that Mai would take care of domestic chores like laundry, cleaning, and cooking, which he disliked doing. The next two evenings they spent quietly at the villa, not doing much, simply enjoying being together. As they sat on the tiled steps, the back garden seemed so secluded. In the near silence, Kendell enjoyed his chilled beer, his arm around Mai's shoulders, and he told her he'd miss her when she went back to town. "I wish you could stay longer."

"I like to stay too," she said. "It's very nice to be here with you. But I have to work and study. Make money and think about future." All of these thoughts and feelings danced around in Kendell's mind for the whole weekend, so, early on Monday morning, during breakfast that Mai had prepared, he finally suggested that she live with him.

"There's no need to work at Mimi's. You can still go to your classes. I can give you fifty thousand every month, and you won't need to rent a room in Saigon anymore."

Mai was beaming as she heard this, but remained quiet for a few seconds before saying, "Okay, honey, let me think. It difficult to decide, because it serious subject. Can you come to Saigon, Friday night? I will let you know."

After breakfast, she drove Kendell on back of the Honda to the bus stop, and he felt a bit self-conscious sitting behind her, looking over the top of her conical hat. He squeezed her shoulders, got off, and she turned in the direction of Saigon. He'd already noticed that the bundle wasn't tied to the bike now, and that she'd left some of her clothes at the villa.

At the motor pool, Kendell told Ralph about his offer to Mai. Ralph said that he'd seen her in Mimi's and he thought she was pretty. He said that some guys had tried to take her out, but she'd never go with them. He thought she was probably looking for a husband.

Ralph was correct in his assessment. In fact, Kendell knew less about Mai than she did about him.

***

Her full name was Khanh Thi Mai, from the city of Dong Ha in Quang Tri Province. She was born there in 1945, into a middle class, educated family. Her parents spoke French and were teachers. Her father taught at the University of Hue. She had an older sister and a younger brother. They had a modest bungalow with a telephone, a small Renault car, and employed a servant.

Mai married at nineteen to a boy from a similar background, while they were both in college. Her husband was conscripted into the South Vietnamese Army and assigned to an infantry battalion. He'd been wounded and recovered physically, but his behavior had changed, which was evident on his home visits. He was now drinking, smoking, and gambling, and they were always short of money because of these vices, especially the gambling. They frequently argued, and he became threatening towards her. They couldn't afford their own place, so they stayed with her parents.

Two years into the marriage, Mai gave birth to a son, but her husband never got to see the boy, as he was killed in action. In 1965, when the Americans poured more troops into

Vietnam, the family's fortunes took yet another turn for the worse. Her brother went missing in action, and her father was detained and tortured by the Viet Cong while on a visit to his parents' village. He was traumatized by this, and could no longer work. Her mother still taught in high school for a very small wage, but it was barely enough to sustain the household. Then, Mai's brother-in-law got drafted into the army. He too, earned little, and was constantly away.

The family sold the car and other possessions in order to keep going, but they kept the telephone. Mai's sister took to selling vegetables in front of the house. Her father, mother, and sister were loving towards her son, as the boy was the only brightness in this decimated family, but, by the time he turned three years old, Mai had had enough. Desperate, she decided to go down to Saigon to get work and make money. There was no chance of this in Quang Tri.

In the city, she initially stayed in a room with a friend from school. This girl, Phan, worked at the London bar on Tu Do Street. She told Mai everything about it, and that she made good money from going out with the foreign customers. Mai told her that she'd try it for a while because she was desperate, but she didn't want to sell her body. Phan suggested Mimi's … lots of American civilians hung out there, and the girls were pretty and classy, and Mai could still make some money without actually sleeping with the customers. Mai was interviewed by Madam Mimi herself, and was told that she could start work immediately.

Chapter 9

At home in Saigon

It was Friday night, and Kendell was back in Saigon for the first time since he'd moved to Thu Duc. He remembered what Tom Clarke, the area supervisor, had suggested, and he got a room at Zack's Place on Tran Quy Cap Street. After the bus arrived, he'd hailed a pedicab and went directly there.

Zack's was owned by Walt Zachary, a 45-year-old black American from New York. He was a musician and singer, and a veteran of the entertainment circuit in Asia. He'd played in military clubs, hotels, nightclubs, and bars all over the Far East. He was tall, friendly, funny, and had a beaming smile. One of his upper front teeth was missing, and he usually had a lit cigarette lodged in the gap. The place was a converted three-story shophouse. The ground level was a bar and restaurant serving up soul food prepared by Walt's Vietnamese wife. The upper two floors were a mini hotel. There was a piano in the bar, and Walt would play and sing if the bar was busy. Most of the customers thought that he sounded like Nat King Cole, but most were unaware that Walt didn't really sound like the great singer … it was all just part of his act.

Kendell left his overnight bag in his room, then went downstairs, where Walt was behind the bar counter, serving drinks.

"Welcome to Zack's shack," Walt said, as Kendell took a stool. "First one on the house."

Kendell said thanks and ordered a cold Hamm's, and soon got talking to Walt and a couple of other characters who were taking advantage of the early evening happy hour.

It was 9:30 by the time Kendell got to Mimi's, where he was slightly annoyed to find Mai already sitting with an older customer. Kendell felt a twinge of jealousy, but reminded himself that she was just doing her job. He sat at the bar and ordered a Hamm's, hoping that the old guy would leave quickly.

It wasn't long before Jay Chastain and Kevin Garsten walked in and took seats next to Kendell, who shook hands with both of them and was glad of the company while Mai wasn't available.

"Haven't seen you in town lately," said Jay. "How's the new house?"

"All good," Kendell replied. "I'm just in town for the night. Staying at Zack's Place. It seems okay."

Kevin said, "Great place. I love Walt. I live just three doors down on the same side, and Jay has a room right across the street." He pointed to Kendell's beer. "You ready for another?"

As they drank and talked, Kendell kept glancing over at Mai, sitting with her customer. She looked back at him, smiling and raising her eyebrows every now and then, trying not to be too obvious. Finally, after what seemed like an age, the guy paid up and left, and Mai came right over to Kendell. "Sorry, honey, it so busy tonight," she whispered to him."

"I'll get back to you guys in a bit," Kendell said to Jay and Kevin, then took his drink and guided Mai over to the sofas.

They sat, he ordered her a Saigon tea, and she spoke first: "You know, I think all week about what you say, and I do want to stay with you. But you know how much money I make here, and I need that for my future."

Kendell had already thought out the money aspect. After three months of his trial employment, he'd get a fifteen percent salary increase. This was a bit more than enough to cover what she earned at the bar, and he figured that Clara didn't need to know about this rise. "Like I said, I can give you fifty thousand P at the end of every month. And you can keep going to school if you want. I'll buy all the food, if you don't mind cooking and taking care of the house."

She didn't respond for a minute, as she thought it over. Then her serious expression turned into a big smile. She hugged Kendell and gave him a long kiss on his cheek. "Alright, honey, I will tell Mimi that I want to finish here, but I still work until she can find another girl."

Kendell was hoping he'd made the right move, but said, "Good, we need to celebrate." He ordered her another drink, then said, "I'm staying at Zack's Place tonight. You can stay there with me."

"I would like to go with you, honey, but I never stay that kind of place. That where people go for short time."

Kendell was disappointed because he was in the mood to sleep with her but, at the same time, he was impressed that she had, and stood by, her principles.

Mai said, "Don't worry, honey. You just go work every day, and when Mimi get new girl, I will come to villa. I bring things with me. Not sure what day, but soon."

"Okay, sounds good." He kissed her on the cheek. "I think I'll go back to Zack's with these boys. I have to get up early for the bus, anyway."

He called for his bill, paid, gave Mai a hug, then rejoined Jay and Kevin at the bar. "You guys want a last call at Zack's? I'm buying."

***

Fifteen minutes later, the three of them were at Zack's, which was busy by now – meaning that Walt was seated at the piano. There were two soldiers, wearing berets, drinking at the bar, whom Kevin recognized. In fact, he didn't like one of them, named Morgan, a Special Forces sergeant who often bragged about Vietnamese people that he'd killed. Kevin had been in the Air Force as a non-combatant, and couldn't stand the bluster and arrogance of some of the "killer" types like Morgan. Kevin liked the Vietnamese people, and was about to marry his long-time Saigon girlfriend.

Jay soon had his eye on two nice-looking girls sharing a tall beer at a table. They both smiled at him and, shortly, he and Kendell were sitting drinking with them, while Kevin stayed at the bar.

Walt was crooning along, doing his best Lou Rawls impression, as the place buzzed with laughter, singing, conversation, and glasses clinking. Then there was a sudden crash and a ruckus at the bar. Stools had been knocked over as Kevin and Morgan stood up and angrily faced each other, and the room went silent.

"Fuck you," shouted Kevin.

Morgan instantly swung and connected with a big punch to Kevin's face. Kevin immediately dropped hard, onto his back. He was out cold, but Morgan started to kick him.

As soon as Walt had seen them square off, he had reached under his seat cushion for the .45 automatic he kept there. "Stop!" he shouted at Morgan, who hesitated, fists clenched, glaring at Walt.

Walt quickly closed the distance to Morgan, the big pistol pointed straight at his forehead. "You lay another finger on him, it'll be the last thing you ever do, you fucking bastard. Think I'm joking…? Just make a move." He kept an eye on Morgan's buddy, who still sat at the bar. The cigarette had fallen out from the gap in Walt's teeth.

Morgan's pal got slowly down from his stool as Walt took a step back so that he could cover both of them with his aim. They moved to the doorway and Morgan hissed, "Fucking civilians, you haven't heard the last of this." And the two went out.

Walt bolted the door from the inside and turned his attention to Kevin, who was coming round. Walt's wife came in with ice and towels to help clean up Kevin's bloody face, and Jay and Kendell helped him to his feet. He needed to get stitched up, but he just wanted another beer.

"Screw it," Walt boomed. "Drinks on the house!" He lit a fresh Salem and placed it into the gap in his teeth.

Someone handed Kevin a fresh beer, and he slowly asked Walt, "Would you really have shot that fucker?"

"God damn right," said Walt, as a cluster of patrons watched and listened. "I would have. But … you know … someone left this gun behind, and I've never fired it or even cleaned it. Hell, I don't even know if it's loaded." He pointed the pistol upward with his right hand and pulled the slide back with his left to check it. The slide came off in his hand and fell to the floor. Walt stood there holding the pistol grip, trigger housing, and not much more. Everyone was still in stunned silence.

"Oops…. Maybe it's a good thing I didn't have to use this baby tonight!"

***

Mai's move-in with Kendell took place in stages. About a week after the episode at Zack's, she surprised him again at the villa as he returned from work. She was waiting for him on her motorbike, this time with a medium-sized travel bag strapped to the back. He helped her with her things into the house, and then they got right to it in the bedroom, not having been this close for two weeks. Mai was very passionate and Kendell loved it.

Later, they sat on the sofa and Mai said that Mimi had found a replacement for her, and she was done working there. This had Kendell smiling, but then she said something that surprised him. "You know, I need go Thu Duc police station. I cannot stay with foreigner without police letter. I need to show your passport and they give me paper for you to sign. This called *giay hong thu*. Maybe need to pay eight hundred P."

This was news to Kendell. He knew nothing of this regulation, and wasn't sure how to respond, or if it was even true. "Okay," he replied, after a moment's thought. "I can sign the paper. And you can show my passport … but let me check this with my boss, before you go to the police."

She seemed to accept this, and then busied herself sorting out her belongings and preparing a rice dish for them in the kitchen.

At work the next day, Kendell asked Ralph about this police letter. Ralph told him yes, it was true that Vietnamese weren't permitted to live with foreigners, unless they registered that fact with the police. Both parties had to agree and sign a co-habitation permit – which must have been the word she'd mentioned last night.

Ralph added, "Yeah, and with this permit, if a child is born, the foreigner becomes the registered father on the birth certificate, even if he isn't married to the mother. Otherwise the baby would be a bastard. Keep in mind, some of these gals try to get knocked up, hoping the guy will marry her."

Kendell realized that he still had a lot to learn about Vietnam. "Thanks, Ralph. I'm getting it … slowly," he said.

That night, Mai produced the co-habitation permit form, and they both signed it. She would take it back to the police for certification, and she assured him that she wouldn't leave the passport at the station. The police just wanted to see it and record his particulars.

***

It was the beginning of the rainy season in southern Vietnam, and they were enjoying their evenings together in the quiet villa. Early each morning, Mai went to the market in town to buy fresh food for cooking, and usually had dinner ready for Kendell when he got back. Afterwards, they would listen to music, and Mai would often study her books, while Kendell drank beer, one can after another. Mai didn't like his drinking, but hadn't yet complained about it. She would sometimes have one or two with him, but wasn't really into alcohol. Often, while sitting on the sofa, with the rain peppering the rooftop, Kendell would remove her pajama top and ask her to go to the fridge. It excited him to watch her nice breasts as she walked around in her bikini panties. This invariably resulted in them having sex, either on the sofa or in the bedroom, sometimes both.

A routine life was being established. Mai would do the housework while still attending classes three days a week in the city. Kendell would show up for work and make the money at the motor pool. In reality, she had much more to do each day than he did.

The first friction between them came when Kendell invited some of the boys for a card game at the villa. It was a Friday afternoon. Cal Cole had pulled some strings and arranged for all of them to get off work at noon, and had even arranged for use of a company jeep. Tom Clarke and Jay Chastain also came along to play. Kendell had bought several cases of Hamm's, and had it iced down in a big cooler.

Mai didn't seem very happy when the players invaded the villa just after lunch, but she put on her best front to serve them beer and snacks. Gambling of this sort was illegal in Vietnam, and there was always the threat of police raids. She knew this, and it made her nervous, but none of the men seemed concerned.

It was just a friendly game of five card draw, in piastres. They used chips with an ante limit of 200 per round. Kendell had some country music tapes for the reel-to-reel, and these suited everyone. They all drank as they played, but only Jay and Cal smoked. They were also the two who tended to fold their cards early. Tom seldom did, and it was more of a contest between him and Kendell, with Tom having the winning edge. He often drew three of a kind, a flush, or a straight.

Just before 7:00 p.m., they wound it up, and Cal said, "Let's hit Mimi's for one or two when we get to town." Jay and Tom were in agreement, with Tom designated as driver, as he was the most sober of the three. Kendell felt like he wanted to join them, but he knew that would have caused problems with Mai.

As soon as the three men drove off, Mai asked, "Did you win money?"

"I think I lost a bit," he replied. "Maybe about thirty thousand P, but it was fun."

Mai shot back, "Why you do this? It not smart to throw away money!"

Kendell was taken aback by her outburst. He had no idea that she despised gambling. To him, the money was insignificant, but obviously, he now realized, it wasn't that way with her. He made a mental note … in future penny ante games, he'd tell her that he'd won a little … or at least that he'd broken even.

Mai didn't cook for him that evening. He had to eat some remaining *cha gio* spring rolls that she'd put on the table earlier for the players. She retreated to the bedroom and shut the door, leaving Kendell on the sofa with his country music and beer. He never made it to join her in the bedroom, as he passed out where he was.

In the morning, he woke to the smell of coffee. *She's at least making breakfast for me,* he thought, as he got up from the sofa to go for his shower.

***

Ralph was always the one Kendell would seek out for advice about Vietnam. Ralph had been in the country for years, was married to a Vietnamese lady, and they had three children together. Kendell mentioned Mai's concern about money.

Ralph said, "Listen, man … there are people in this country that don't even earn three thousand piastres each month. There's money in Saigon, but out there in the provinces, they have next to nothing, and are lucky if they grow their own food. Practically every one of the bargirls here is sending money back home. It might be for a kid, or parents, but you can rest assured that they're all supporting someone."

Kendell liked to drink beer back in California, but it was a bit of a luxury for him there, because of his low wages. Here, in Vietnam, it was affordable in the duty-free post exchanges, and maybe that was the reason for the limit of three cases per month. This was nowhere near enough for his needs.

He found out from Cal that there was a Chinese shop-owner who had unlimited supply, but charged a 100 percent black-market premium, on top of the PX price. Even so, it was still cheaper than in the USA.

Kendell received his first order for ten cases of Falstaff, and it was delivered right to his doorstep in the evening. It cost 48 dollars, and he paid with a fifty dollar bill and told the driver to keep the change.

So then, the next problem arose between Kendell and Mai. She didn't mind him having a few drinks at night, but it was very disappointing for her to see him getting drunk often. It was starting to affect his sexual performance, and her interest in it.

"Why you drink so much, honey? That not good. Just waste money and not healthy for you. Better slow, slow. I like you when not drunk."

"Yeah, yeah, okay," Kendell would say, and cut down for a few days, but then get right back into it. When he went over the limit, he would start singing along, loudly, to whatever song was playing on the Panasonic. When drunk, he often tried to get Mai to go half- or fully-naked in the house. This is something she would have readily done if Kendell would stick to reasonable consumption. The villa had dimmable lights, and all the windows had swing-close shutters, so she felt comfortable with it, but his intoxication was a turn-off for her.

One rainy night, drunk, Kendell wanted to go out to the back garden to target practice with his Smith & Wesson. Mai was horrified, and pulled him from the door by his arm. "No! You cannot do this! If police come, they take me to police station…. Big problem for me. I'm Vietnamese…." Kendell relented, went to the refrigerator, and got another can.

Still, he was becoming weary of the hangovers, waking up at 5:30 each morning for work. He was sure that his colleagues in the motor pool could smell the alcohol on him in the mornings, like with many of the other Americans on the site, and he really did want to cut back on the drinking. So, one evening, he came up with a plan to keep him busy and to have some fun. The larger of the spare bedrooms had an empty recess in the concrete wall, probably designed for a fitted closet. Kendell then went into the smaller bedroom, turned around, and looked through the door, across the dining room, all the way to the wall recess in the bigger bedroom opposite. It was all in a direct line of sight.

Mai was in the main bedroom listening to Vietnamese songs on her transistor radio. When there was a lull in the rain, Kendell went out and got a sandbag from the ravine. It was soaked and very heavy, but not a problem for him. He went back to get three more, and arranged them in the recess, three of them stacked and the fourth placed vertically on top of them. Then he got a piece of cardboard and drew a rough target on it, and taped it to the upper bag. His indoor shooting range was all set up.

He called Mai to come and see it. Not surprisingly, she didn't like it. "Why you want to do this? It dangerous!"

Kendell was prepared for this. He said, "Look, I promise you I won't get drunk. I need something to do, and I worry about you being alone here. You should know how to protect yourself."

She frowned and shook her head.

Kendell continued, "I'll teach you to shoot. And … you see that target there? Every time you hit that bullseye in the middle … one hundred P for you…. Don't worry, we'll only practice once in a while."

She gave a nod of approval, but without enthusiasm. "Okay, we try this another night.

I want you to come to bed with me now, honey."

***

The domestic situation showed some improvement and, with Kendell's instruction, Mai agreed to learn how to fire the revolver. Before they started, he asked her to go outside and walk some distance away from the house and listen while he fired a test shot. She returned and reported that the sound wasn't very loud or alarming, and the guards near the road probably wouldn't hear it. However, he had already noted one problem, and when he fired another shot inside the villa, the loud report made their ears ring, so he shut it down. The next evening, he returned with two sets of ear protectors from the motor pool, and they got started.

Mai's initial reluctance was replaced by a keen interest after she began shooting. Her marksmanship quickly improved, and soon she was scoring hits in the middle, which cost Kendell each time. So, in the interest of savings, he made up some new targets with a smaller bullseye. But that ruse didn't work. Once or twice a week, they would have an evening shooting competition, which Mai almost always won because she took it seriously and liked the cash prize incentive. Kendell's drinking was also a factor, as he'd slowly been backsliding on his promises, and wasn't a very good shot after a few cans.

Mai was often exuberant after her wins, when Kendell had to pay up. He didn't mind, because she often became amorous, as well, and would sometimes come back from the kitchen with a beer for him, wearing nothing at all. "Do you like what I bring for you, honey?" she would say, knowing so well that he did.

***

On what should have been a routine morning for Kendell at the motor pool, another tragic incident took place. One of his men, named Hai, was taking apart a big truck tire with a split rim. He'd followed procedure and bled the air pressure, but was unaware that a piece of foreign matter within the tire had clogged the valve stem, trapping pressure inside. He'd removed most of the bolts that held the rim halves together, until there were just four remaining. When Hai began to loosen one of them, all four sheared off, causing a violent explosion.

Kendell was in his office when he heard the blast. He rushed out into the work bay to see a cloud of red dust drifting off, into the wind, from the tire shop. He ran over and was jolted by what he saw. Hai was laying crumpled on the concrete floor, half of his head missing, and his broken body bled out. The floor was awash in blood and inner parts. Some of the shop hands stood at a distance, not wanting to go near the body. Kendell was nauseous, struggling to keep from vomiting. Hai had been his lead man in the tire shop, and Kendell had come to like and respect him. Now he was just a heap of shattered flesh on the floor.

Ralph and Bob Keller soon appeared. Keller was as shocked as Kendell, but Ralph, who had witnessed similar or worse scenes in the Special Forces, immediately took charge of the situation. He called Area Security on the radio, but they had heard the blast and were already on the way. Before long, an ambulance from the Army Evacuation Hospital showed up, and took away Hai's remains in a body bag. A fire truck also arrived, and soon the shop floor was being hosed down and scrubbed clean of the blood and gore … all of it washed down into a storm drain outside. The only trace left of Hai was his civilian shirt, left hanging on a peg at the rear of the shop.

Ralph brought Kendell back to his office to console him. "Listen, a lot of nasty stuff happens in this country. It's not your fault. Let's go up to the club at lunchtime. I'll buy you a drink and you don't have to work this afternoon. My driver will take you home. I'll fill out the report for security." He knew that Kendell was traumatized.

At the club, Kendell wasn't interested in eating. He drank two beers and said to Ralph, "I'm coming back to work with you. I'm alright now."

In fact, he wasn't alright, and felt like staying at the club to get drunk, but he knew that wouldn't look good to others, and he didn't want to show weakness. So, he went back to the shop and did his paperwork and, later in the afternoon, Kevin Garsten came by and helped Kendell to write and sign the fatal incident report.

After work, as soon as he got back to the villa, Kendell immediately started drinking, one beer after another. Mai asked him why he was drinking so much, so quickly, but he refused to tell her anything about what had happened. She had prepared fried noodles, but he didn't want any of it, so she went off to the bedroom and her books, saddened and confused. It was the beginning of a new evening trend for him … even more drinking and less eating. That night, he passed out on the sofa. Mai came out and covered him with a light blanket, then went back to bed by herself.

Kendell's routine went on for weeks, which turned into months. His promise to Mai that he would reduce his drinking was not kept. On some nights when he wasn't hitting it heavily, they would play music, have dinner, and retire to the bedroom for sexual intimacy and sleep. Kendell had lost interest in the shooting range, but he and Mai would occasionally fire off a few rounds, just to keep in practice. Tom, Jay, and Cal came by several times to play cards but, afterwards, Mai would always give Kendell a hard time about gambling.

Kendell knew that he was drinking way too much, that his attempts to control it were pathetic and half-hearted. Some nights he would have just one or two and get along well with Mai, but sometimes there were events at Area 208 that he didn't want to deal with, and the alcohol at night helped him to ignore it.

One afternoon, Kendell and Bob Keller took a jeep ride to the far end of the depot, to check on a crane that had stopped running. Along the way, they noticed some female laborers, gathered in a frantic group, at the steel beam yard. They saw that the first-aid jeep was on the scene. All of the women were clustered around and crouched over one of their friends laying on the ground behind a truck. Most of them were crying and wailing. It was the pretty young storekeeper of the yard. Her *nón lá* was beside her, and her white tunic was crimson with blood. She had obviously suffered severe injuries, and showed no signs of life. A medic told Keller that she'd been standing with her clipboard behind the five-ton truck. The engine was off, and the driver had set the parking brake, but it had failed. When the driver got out, the truck rolled backwards, crushing the girl against a stack of beams, killing her almost instantly.

For the remainder of the day, Kendell couldn't focus on his work at all. He could only think of the girl laying bloodied and lifeless on the ground. The amount of violence and tragedy that he'd seen in only a short time in Vietnam was causing him a great deal of anxiety, although he wasn't fully aware of it. It was making him irritable and tense, except when he was drinking, which was now almost his only pastime.

Even during the daytime at work, his habit was worsening. At lunch, at the club, either with Ralph or any of the other guys, or alone, he would down two or three beers with his food, which was invariably served by the pretty Cambodian waitress, whom he was now paying more attention to. He found that it helped him through the afternoon, until he could get back to the villa for more. He always tipped the waitress and, when he did, she would smile and flirt a bit with him. One day, as Kendell was about to leave the club, she placed a folded piece of paper in front of him and said, "You look later." He put the paper in his shirt pocket and, once back in his office, took it out and read her message: "My name is Tam. You look like good man. If you want meet me, my day off is Friday. This my phone number in Bien Hoa 6178023. Must ask for Tam. Hope see you sometime."

Kendell tore up the message but, before doing so, he copied the number on a piece of paper and placed it in his wallet. He was, after all, attracted to her.

Chapter 10

Dong Ha Trip

In early November, Mai received a letter that made it urgent to call her family in Dong Ha. First, she tried from the phone at the villa, but it was useless. She had to call the operator to get a connection, but twice it didn't work. The third time, the operator didn't even bother calling back. It was typical of the system, and, in the end, she went to the Central Post Office, where the connections were more reliable.

When she got through, her mother told her that her father was in need of an operation. He'd been having some pain near his liver, and an X-ray showed that he had a tumor, so the surgery was scheduled for the end of the month. Her mother said that it could be life threatening, or turn out to be not so serious, depending on the findings. Mai said she would try to get home in time for his hospitalization. She didn't know how much the operation would cost, but she had kept almost all of what Kendell had been giving her each month, and hoped that her savings would be enough to cover the cost; after all, it was at a government-subsidized hospital.

On one of the nights that Kendell wasn't fully intoxicated, Mai told him about her father, and that she had to go home. "I want to go, end of this month, and will stay one week. Is that okay, honey?"

To her surprise, Kendell agreed straight away. "How will you get there?" he asked.

"I will fly. Air Vietnam. Not so expensive. Maybe only eighteen thousand P."

Kendell did the math. "About eighty dollars…. Okay, I'll pay for you. It'll be good for you to see your family."

In actuality, Kendell was looking forward to a break from Mai. She had been annoying him with her frequent criticism of his drinking and gambling, but, in his alcoholic state of mind, he couldn't realize that Mai was only concerned with his well-being, and what was good for him and their relationship. Kendell appreciated none of this, and interpreted it as nagging.

In the days leading up to Mai's trip back home, Kendell asked Bob Keller if he could take off for a few days. He hadn't taken any sick leave so far, so Keller agreed to give him four days off, on the condition that Ralph would also agree to it and cover for Kendell while he was away. Kendell had already briefed Ralph, who said it that wouldn't be a problem, so the deal was on.

Mai planned to leave on a Wednesday, so Kendell asked for the Thursday through Sunday, and to report back to work on the Monday morning. He would go to Saigon to spend a few days and do a bit of unwinding, but he didn't mention any of this to Mai.

It was still dark at six in the morning of Mai's departure, and she was packed and ready to go. Kendell locked the villa door and carried her bag as they walked out to the highway. It was cool and damp, and birds were beginning to chirp in the trees. At the highway, the old public bus for Saigon was taking on passengers. Kendell squeezed both of Mai's hands as they gazed at each other. "You take care, and have a safe trip. I hope your father gets well," he said. Mai turned and blew a kiss to him as she clambered up the steps.

That night, back at the villa, Kendell prepared a few clothing and toiletry items to take to Saigon in the morning. He could have brought these things to the office that morning, and gone directly to Saigon after work, but Mai would have noticed and realized what he was up to.

On Thursday morning, Kendell was out on the highway at 7:30 to catch the company bus, bringing the night shift back to Saigon. In town, he got off with his tote bag and walked the short distance to the Catinat Hotel for breakfast. The coffee was still terrible, but the toasted French bread with black-peppered scrambled eggs and fried bacon with onions was just what he needed. The old waiter in his long-sleeved white shirt remembered him, and Kendell left him a 200-piastre tip.

Next stop was Zack's Place, so Kendell hailed a Renault taxi for the ride.

When he got there, he found Walt scowling over some paperwork in the bar; the gun-slinging crooner was alone except for the cleaning lady, who was tidying up from the previous night's festivities.

"Good to see you, Walt," said Kendell. "I need a room for three nights."

"No problem. Two thousand per night … but the room needs cleaning; you're a bit early. You want a beer while you're waiting? First one's on me."

"Thanks, I'll take a Falstaff."

A half hour later, his room was ready, so he dumped his bag on the bed and went back out to the street. He wanted to head down to Hai Ba Trung Street, but it was still too early for that scene, so he walked downtown to kill time.

Kendell was sweating by the time he reached Mohan's tailor shop on Tu Do Street. He needed plenty of money for this spree, and in the back room he wrote a personal check for 250 dollars and asked Mohan to give it to him in piastres. This amounted to 55,000. He asked Mohan for two envelopes, into which he split the notes. He then placed one each into the back pockets of his jeans.

After he left the shop, Kendell walked slowly in the direction of the river. As he strolled along the busy Tu Do sidewalk, four adolescent boys came up from behind, crowding him as he continued walking. Two of them got in front of him, close to his face and started talking at him. "Mister, mister, you have cigarette?" one of them said. "Then another: "Mister, you give me American cigarette?" Kendell instinctively covered his front right pocket, where he always carried his wallet. As he was being jostled, he yelled, "No! No cigarettes…. Get the hell away from me!"

The four broke away and disappeared around the corner of a building in a flash. Kendell checked his jeans. His wallet and keys were still in his front pocket, but one of the cash envelopes was gone from his right rear.

"Damn!" He should have seen it coming. There was nothing he could do now. He knew that it was useless to go to the police … even if they rounded up the gang, they might just steal the rest of it. He now recalled his first day in Saigon, when Will Posey had warned him about pick-pockets. He shook his head, decided to cut his losses and continue on to the London bar, which should be open by now.

Once there, he took out the remaining envelope. It contained 27,000 piastres, so the gang had gotten 28,000 with the other envelope … just under 130 dollars. Oh well, Kendell still had a 100-dollar note in his wallet to cover a situation like this.

By early afternoon, the bar was starting to get lively. The girls were nice, but the place was a bit high-end, so he drank up and moved on. He avoided going near Mimi's, where he might be recognized by any of the staff who knew Mai.

On Hai Ba Trung Street, Kendell decided to hit the row of bars from one end to the other. The Tennessee was first on his agenda. It was happy hour … thirty percent discount all day until seven. The daytime girls were chatty and not pushing him to buy drinks. He quickly forgot the episode with the street boys, and focused on the good time he was having. The next bar was even better. Kendell entered it without even noticing the name of the place. It didn't matter. The rock music was great, the girls sexy, and the beers cold.

As the afternoon went by and Kendell consumed more, he got into an ecstatic mood. His natural reticence was replaced by an urge to talk with people … staff and customers alike. A young American soldier asked him what he was doing in Vietnam. He replied, "Working for a contractor and having the time of my life, while getting paid for it." They both laughed and Kendell bought the boy a beer."

And so it went. Kendell's binge was in full progress. Around sunset, in the Ritz bar, he had a thought. He looked into his wallet and found the phone number for Tam, the Cambodian waitress. The Ritz had a telephone, so he asked the mamasan if he could pay to call Bien Hoa . She said no problem, 300 piastres for three minutes. He gave her the number and asked her to get Tam on the line. After a few failed attempts, Mama finally connected with Tam and handed the phone to him.

"Hello, Tam…. This is Kendell … from the 199th club. Are you still off tomorrow? I'm in Saigon. Can you come?"

Tam answered, "Oh … yes. You want me come tonight? I can still get bus. Where you stay?"

That took him by surprise, but it was a tantalizing offer. "Okay, I'm at Zack's Place … Tran Quy Cap Street. Can you remember that? It's a bar and hotel. What time can you be here?"

She replied that she could be there by nine.

"Alright, I'll see you then. Bye."

Kendell turned to buy a drink for the Mama-san. He still had a few hours before he had to get back to Zack's, so he decided to make the most of it. Next stop was the Alaska bar, which didn't disappoint him.

Although he'd been drinking steadily since mid-morning, Kendell wasn't overly intoxicated. Outside the New Orleans bar, he hailed a pedicab and headed back to Zack's. Along the way, he gulped in the cool night air, which helped to sober him a bit. He didn't want to be too out of control when the Cambodian girl arrived.

When Tam walked in at 9:30, Kendell was nursing a bottle of mineral water at the bar. Damn, he thought, this was one pretty lady.

Her eyes were big and expressive, her teeth perfect, her long hair was in a pony-tail, and she had a flawless complexion. She wore no makeup, and he thought she didn't really need it. She was somewhat tall for an Asian woman, and walked upright. She wore jeans and a tight red T-shirt and sandals. Everyone in the bar had noticed her.

Kendell got up and walked a few steps to meet her, took hold of her overnight bag, and led her to a bar stool, where they sat close together. She placed her hand on his thigh, leaned over, and said, "So nice to meet here tonight." He couldn't agree more.

It turned out that Tam liked to drink a bit. She ordered a beer, and Kendell followed suit. Walt wasn't singing yet, but there was mood music on the sound system, and the atmosphere was relaxed. Some of the customers were dining, so Kendell asked Tam if she was hungry. She said that something light would be good, maybe a basket of fried chicken wings and corn bread. They slowly shared the food, drank, and made small talk at the bar, comfortable in each other's company.

When they finished eating, Kendell said, "Do you want to put your things in the room, take a shower, or anything? We can come back down to listen to the singer."

"Yes, we go up," she replied. But they didn't make it back down to the bar that night. After showering, they were all over each other with a passion. Perhaps the months of secretly admiring each other had spilled over into this sexual frenzy. But perhaps it was more than that. People affected by the fear and frustration caused by war sometimes seek reckless outlets for their tensions and desires. It was a 'live as if there's no tomorrow' mentality. But it was likely that Tam understood this more than Kendell.

They slept until the sun was well up. As he woke, Kendell didn't, at first, know where he was, but then the room came into focus and he felt the warmth of Tam's body beside him. He was very thirsty after all the alcohol he'd consumed. He poured a glass of water from the pitcher on the bedside table and gulped it down. Then he drank another glassful before dozing again, not fully asleep. When Tam stirred and turned to him, they were soon embraced again in a way that matched their passions of the previous night.

After they showered together, Tam got dressed and went out to buy food. She was back in ten minutes, carrying large bowls of beef with rice noodles and mint soup, which came from a street vendor and was known to be good for the "morning after."

Kendell was good to go after this breakfast, and he began thinking about a plan for the day. It seemed to him that he had everything he needed right here at Zacks … food, drink, accommodation, and a lovely woman. There really wasn't any reason to go anywhere else. He asked Tam, "What time do you have to go back to Bien Hoa?"

"Evening time," she said. "But if you like me to stay, I can go early tomorrow morning."

That settled it for Kendell. They would spend the whole day and night right there at Zack's.

***

Mid-afternoon, they went down to the bar, where Kendell had his first cold one with Walt. Being a Friday, customers began to show up a bit earlier than usual, and it soon became lively. Some of the men glanced admiringly at Tam, and it gave Kendell a sense of pride that she was with him. He'd made the right decision, asking her to come, and right here, right now, he honestly couldn't think of any place he'd rather be. His life had turned around, and he was grateful for it. It wasn't perfect, but adjustments could be made. The first realizations that he might have made a mistake by getting into a serious live-in relationship, so soon after escaping the confines of his marriage, began to occur to him. He envied the guys he knew who lived the bachelor life in Saigon. He needed to give it some serious thought … but not before this binge was over.

***

On Saturday morning, Tam woke Kendell just as it was getting light. He groaned and opened his eyes. She stood next to the bed, fully dressed, and handed him a cool glass of water. "I go now…. Must work at club later."

Kendell sat up and said, "Oh … hold on a minute." He reached for his jeans. "Here, take some money for a taxi." He handed her 2,000 piastres.

"Thank you," she said. "Bye-bye, see you soon." She leaned over to kiss him, then turned and went out.

Kendell decided to sleep in. He had overdone the drinking, and was tired from that and his exertions with Tam. When he woke again at noontime, he went down and had a late breakfast of Spanish omelet, coffee, and toast. That revived him but, without Tam there, he didn't feel like spending his day at Zack's, so he found himself back on Hai Ba Trung Street, drinking at the Alaska in the early afternoon. On Saturdays, things got going early on, and soon Kendell was enjoying himself, bantering with the bar staff and customers, buying Saigon teas, and hopping from bar to bar.

He carried on until around eight, then decided he should get back to Zack's while he was still in control. Once there, though, he got a second wind and downed a few more Hamm's with Walt and some others before calling it a night. The plan was to ease off on Sunday and catch the evening bus back to Thu Duc. He needed to be at work on Monday morning.

Chapter 11

Welcome home

Mai arrived in the early afternoon. Things in Dong Ha had gone better than expected. The result of her father's operation was favorable; the tumor turned out to be a benign cyst, and was successfully removed. Her boy was healthy and doing well, although he seemed closer to Mai's parents than to herself. But the surgery had cost more than she had in savings, so she had borrowed the deficit from a money lender. It had to be repaid within seven days, in order to avoid the high interest, so she returned to Saigon early, to get her end-of-month stipend from Kendell and send back what she owed.

As Kendell got down from the bus at Thu Duc at 6:30, he realized that he felt quite good, despite his excesses in town. He'd had three final drinks at the Catinat before getting on the bus, so that might have given him a boost. It was dark already as he walked along the lane towards the villa, but then, within sight of it, he stopped in his tracks. The lights were on and he heard faint Vietnamese music coming from the radio within. Oh, Jesus …

she's back. He took a minute, leaned against a palm tree, and thought about what he was going to say. Alright, I can handle this, he convinced himself, and walked up to the front door.

It was bolted from inside, and he had to knock … but with no response for a couple of minutes.

"Mai, please open the door," he called.

Eventually, it opened, and she stood there in one of his long T-shirts. She didn't smile or say anything. One look at him, she knew that he'd been drinking, and heavily. She also knew, from looking around the villa, that he hadn't been there in days. At first, she'd been worried, thinking that something might have happened to him at work, but now that he'd showed up in this condition, an hour earlier than usual, she immediately knew that he'd been to Saigon.

"You wait for me to go home, then you go have big party for yourself," she said quietly. "When I first meet you, I think you honest man, but I wrong about you."

"They gave me some time off," he said. "It's too boring staying here alone, so I went to Saigon… and, anyway, I needed to get some money changed."

"You think I'm stupid," she said in a raised voice. "Yes, maybe I'm stupid to be with you. I know I cannot trust shit man like you."

He was already irritated, even though he knew he deserved her scorn. He went to the refrigerator and got a Falstaff, which he opened and began drinking.

Mai then yelled at him, "You only care about yourself. You don't need someone like me. I always care for you, but you too drunk and stupid. You don't know anything."

"Calm down. What in hell is wrong with you?" said Kendell.

Mai shouted back to him, "Where is my money for last month? You say you get money changed in Saigon. I need now … it important."

Kendell replied, "You won't believe this, but on Tu Do Street, some boys picked my pocket and stole 28,000 piastres from me."

Upon hearing this, Mai broke into a loud rant in Vietnamese. To Kendell, it seemed that she was becoming hysterical, so he decided it would be a good time to go for a shower.

When he came back out to the kitchen, Mai was sobbing at the table, with her head down upon her forearms. She tearfully looked up at him, in his shorts, shirtless. Low on his neck, near his collarbone, she saw two love bites that he hadn't even realized were there. This was too much for her, and her instinctive reaction was to reach for the sugar bowl and hurl it at him.

Kendell dodged the missile, which shattered against the wall.

Now he'd had enough. "You know, you're acting like a crazy bitch. I don't need this. Tomorrow I want you out of here … out! I can't live like this. You take all your things and go. This is too much."

Mai sobbed deeply and ran off into the bedroom.

Kendell was very agitated. He spun around and went to the refrigerator to grab another beer.

Just moments later, Mai came out from the bedroom. "Kendell!" she screamed.

Holding the unopened can, he turned to face her, and froze in disbelief…. She stood, wide-eyed, still in tears, pointing the Smith & Wesson directly at him.

"Mai," he said, slowly and calmly.

But it would be the last word he ever uttered. There was a thunderclap and a blinding flash in his face … the instant, final vision of his life.

Kendell was dead as he hit the floor, shot though the heart.

Chapter 12

Mitigation

At work on Monday morning, Ralph Gates was aware that Kendell hadn't showed up on the bus, as he reliably did each day. Ralph knew that Kendell had been hitting the bars in Saigon on his four-day fling, and figured that the guy might have just overslept and missed his ride. The motor pool had a military phone system. To call Kendell at home, Ralph would have had to go over to Kevin Garsten's office at the operations building, which could link into the public system. It was a bit complicated, and the connections were always bad or non-existent, so he decided to wait, half-expecting Kendell to roll in late and looking the worse for wear.

As lunchtime approached, Kendell still hadn't appeared, so Ralph walked over to the ops building and found Kevin at the security office.

"Hey, Kevin. I don't know if there's a problem, but Kendell hasn't showed up today. He's never missed a day so far. Maybe we'd better check up on him. What do you think?"

Kevin said, "Yeah, okay, let's try calling his place. You got his home number?"

After a couple of failed attempts, he said, "I'll try again later. If I can't get through, Todd's heading to the main office in town … I'll have him stop by at Kendell's place on the way. I'm having lunch here today, so I'll get back to you as soon as I hear something."

***

Mid-afternoon, Kevin walked into the motor pool office and approached Ralph. "Got some terrible news, Ralph. We couldn't get through on the phone, so Todd and his driver stopped over there to check. The front door wasn't locked, so they went in. They found him on the kitchen floor … dead. It looks like a shooting, and it probably happened last night. His body was stiff."

"Oh, Christ," said Ralph. "Who shot him?"

"We're working on it," Kevin said. "Todd got the Thu Duc police to come in, along with the Regional Forces guards from the main gate. But they're useless, as you know. We got the Evac Hospital people to clean up and take care of the body. I'm waiting for Will to get out to Thu Duc. Todd and I are going back down there to meet him at Kendell's place."

"This is terrible," said Ralph. "And it's going to cause a shitload of problems."

***

Todd and Kevin's driver pulled up in front of the villa just before 5:00 pm. One of the Regional Force security guards was standing not far away, keeping an eye on things. Minh's Datsun was parked outside, and Will Posey was sitting, smoking, on the front steps in the late afternoon light. He nodded at Todd and Kevin, then shook his head and said, "Alright guys, let's go inside and analyze this mess."

Posey motioned for Todd and Kevin to sit with him at the dining room table. Looking at Kevin, he said, "Check the fridge … see if there's any beer. I wasn't planning on spending happy hour in Thu Duc, but here we are."

Kevin put two Falstaffs on the table, and a Coke for Todd, who didn't drink beer.

Posey opened his can and continued, "The police have the gun. They found it in the bedroom … just one shot fired. They'll be taking prints off it. Their report will be finished tomorrow … in Vietnamese, of course. The Evac Hospital will have the coroner's report soon, but they've already called us and said the cause of death was a gunshot wound to the heart. Looks like his fucking girlfriend shot him!"

"What the hell happened?" Kevin pondered out loud.

"We don't know. Might have been jealousy … money … maybe self-defense. The police will find her and she'll talk … they'll make sure of that. By the way, Todd, good that you were here when the cops arrived, otherwise they probably would have walked away with whatever they wanted from this place."

Kevin got up and said, "You guys know about his indoor shooting range…? Jay Chastain told me about it." He went over to the doorway of the spare bedroom. Posey and Todd joined him. They all peered inside and saw the propped-up sandbags against the far wall, with a bullet-ridden homemade target attached to it.

"I'll be God-damned!" Posey exclaimed. "And did he teach his girlfriend how to shoot?"

Todd said, "Yeah, he did, and I've heard she was a pretty good shot … which is now obvious."

Posey responded, "Fuck me, I can't believe this crazy bastard would actually teach his girlfriend how to shoot! Why the fuck didn't he live in town like the rest of us … where you naturally wouldn't have a fucking shooting range in your apartment?"

He took a long drink from his beer can, then went on, "Okay, Todd, you arrange for all of his personal effects to be sent to the main office warehouse. Make double sure none of the girlfriend's clothing, or whatever, gets included. All this stuff has to be shipped to his wife in California. Minh knows the landlord of this place … he'll have let him know that he'll be needing a new tenant!"

Kevin asked, "What do you want me to do?"

"I think you know already," Posey replied. "This can't get out as murder. Then I'd have to deal with the asshole State Department officials at the embassy, and that would be a fucking nightmare."

The two others nodded in agreement at that sentiment.

"It could also affect the status of our contracts," Posey continued. "And we're not going to let that happen. I'm sending Minh to negotiate a deal with the Thu Duc police, to give us the kind of report we need. Kevin, you're a good writer … I'm leaving it to you to do a fatal incident report, and a letter to Kendell's wife. We'll wire it to the LA office. They'll type it up and send a rep to personally hand it to the wife and give her our condolences. Run them by me as soon as possible, tomorrow, before we release it."

The three men went out the door and stood on the patio in the light of the descending sun. Todd had found the door keys on the coffee table. He locked up and put them in his pocket. "What now?"

Posey replied, "You guys send your jeep back to 208. You're both riding with me and Minh back to Saigon. We're going to Hai Ba Trung in honor of Kendell. Poor bastard would have loved to be with us."

***

The Thu Duc police had Mai's residential details from the registration form for the co-habitation permit to live with Kendell. The listed address was that of her parents' house in Dong Ha. They telegraphed their counterparts there, requesting apprehension of Mai under suspicion of murder. Dong Ha sent an officer to the address, but Mai's family told him that she had left for Saigon a few days before.

One of the Thu Duc cops then contacted Minh, and asked if Kendell's girlfriend had worked any bars. Minh told them to check

Mimi's, so they contacted the Saigon police for assistance.

At first, Madam Mimi didn't want to cooperate, but the Saigon cops threatened her with aiding a fugitive, so she relented and gave them Mai's address on Nguyen Trai Street. All along, Mai had kept the rented room, without telling Kendell. It was cheap, near to her classes, and it was a backup if their relationship didn't work. There, the police found and arrested her. She'd gone back, in a state of shock and remorse, not realizing how easily she'd be tracked down. The Saigon police were overwhelmed with work, as usual, and didn't want to deal with the case, so they called Thu Duc to come and get her.

***

The Thu Duc station soon exonerated Mai in their special report, negotiated with Minh for 60,000 piastres. Will Posey maintained a 'dark money' cash reserve for exactly this kind of transaction. The Thu Duc police captain, however, knowing who the true killer was, decided to make Mai's time with them very unpleasant, to see what further could be gained from her. The captain took her into an interrogation room and pressured her to give him oral sex. She violently resisted and screamed so loudly that he had to back off, not wanting the whole station to hear the ruckus. He also figured that if he pursued it, with Mai being so hysterical, she might even do irreparable damage that he wouldn't be able to explain to his wife.

The only thing left for the captain was to get as much money as he could before letting her go. He told Mai that she'd go to prison and perhaps die there unless she could pay to settle the case. She said the only thing she owned was a Honda motorbike, which she could sell for 50,000 piastres. He left her in a filthy, overcrowded cell with the other women prisoners for three days, then told her that she could go as soon as she paid up. He then let her call her money lender in Dong Ha, and she arranged to have the cash wired to her at the Thu Duc post office. A few hours later, he took her there to receive the funds, which she handed right over to him, and then she was free to go.

He gave her a few piastres for bus fare back to the city, but only after she had to ask for it.

Chapter 13

March 29, 2020; Lancaster California

It was only a ten-minute drive to the cemetery, but after parking the truck, they had to walk in for a couple of minutes, through the rows of headstones and crosses, thousands of them.

Kendell's grave was partly shaded by an aspen tree. The ground-level headstone had no special inscription, just his name and dates of birth and death.

Jake and Jenny stood, rather somber, while Clara placed the bunch of flowers on the stone, and then sat on a folding canvas chair that they'd brought for her. The three of them were quiet, all contemplating the past.

After a few minutes of silence, Jake reached into his little six-pack cooler and withdrew two bottles of beer and a Coke for Clara. He placed one beer on the grave, handed one to Jenny, then took another from the cooler for himself.

Four or five rows away, Jenny spotted an older guy they knew vaguely from the Veterans of Foreign Wars Club, and who had served in Vietnam. The man was placing an American flag on a grave.

Jake called out, "Hey … Mike."

Mike looked up and waved. "Yo, Jake." He took a few moments to pay his respects at the headstone, then strolled over to the small congregation.

Jake introduced Mike to his mother, who shook his hand and smiled. Jenny had already met him at the VFW.

"What brings you all here today?" Mike asked.

"Not sure if I told you before," said Jake. "Our father was killed in Vietnam in 1968."

"Oh, I had no idea," Mike replied. "What unit was he in?"

"Well, he wasn't in the military. He was a civilian contractor, but he died as a result of hostile action."

As he said this, Jake raised his eyebrows and rolled his eyes towards Clara. Mike quickly sensed that Jake didn't want to bring up the details at that moment.

"Yeah, I lost quite a few buddies there, too," Mike said. "Charlie Abbott over there," he added, pointing to the grave where he'd placed the flag.

"You want a beer?" Jake offered.

"Sure, why not."

Clara still sat quietly as the three others talked about the VFW Club and the military, and, when they'd finished their beers, Jake said, "Hey, you're welcome to come back to our place for another cold one if you like. Got something to show you ... now I think of it. And we've still got plenty of pancake mix on the stove. Right, Mom?"

"Sounds good," Mike said. "I'll follow you in my car."

***

Back at the house, Clara served up more pancakes as Jake, Jenny, and Mike resumed drinking and talked of military adventures in Afghanistan and Iraq. When Clara retired to the living room to take a nap, the conversation turned to Vietnam, and Mike recounted some of his own stories and what Saigon was like in those wartime days.

"I've heard about the civilians in Vietnam back then, "Jenny said. "It was party time in Saigon. I'm not saying it was all of them, but quite a few were screwing the bargirls like crazy and drinking themselves blind. I think that's why Dad didn't want to live in the city ... it wasn't his style."

"Yeah, he was more of a loner," Jake added. "I think he was just there to make money for us."

"Right," Jenny said. "But if it weren't for his sacrifice and the life insurance, Mom would never have been able to buy this place…. There should be a civilian award for the service of people like him, but there isn't."

Jake then stood and went to the drawer of a side table below the framed photo of Wade. "Take a look at this, Mike."

He withdrew a laminated, single-page document that a representative of AA&E had brought to Clara in 1968, and handed it to Mike.

Mike took out a case from his pocket, put on his glasses, and began reading.

Company notification [Classified]

AA&E

Atlantic Architect and Engineers, 363/22 Plantation Road, Ton Son Nhut 1755, Saigon, Republic of South Vietnam. Tel: 01- 755655

December 2, 1968

Mrs. Clara Kendell
17 Sage Crest Park
Lancaster, CA
USA.

Dear Mrs. Kendell,

It is with profound sympathy, and that of my colleagues, that we must inform you of the passing of your beloved husband, Wade Thomas Kendell, on the night of December 1, 1968.

"Kendell," as he was known by all of us who knew and respected him, lived by himself in a villa at Thu Duc, not far from our Area 208 work site. The estate where he lived has Regional Forces civilian guards for perimeter security, and Kendell had volunteered to become one of the deputized neighborhood watch officers. As such, he was issued with a handgun.

At approximately 8:15 p.m. on the night in question, Communist Viet Cong infiltrators breached the walls of the estate, intent on assassinating government officials and Americans living there. Kendell was most likely woken by nearby gunfire, and prepared to defend himself and others. At his home, a gunfight ensued between him and some of the attackers. He was wounded, but continued to return gunfire, resulting in the deaths of two Viet Cong, before he succumbed to his own injuries.

Kendell's body was sent to the US Army 93rd Evacuation Hospital, and was blessed by a Christian chaplain. The Coroner's Unit will provide a report, and his body will be flown this week to California, to enable you to make funeral arrangements.

Our Administration Department in Saigon will arrange for all of your husband's personal belongings to be returned to you by air. They will also coordinate with you on all necessary arrangements, as well as his company life insurance policy, as you are the sole beneficiary.

Kendell's dedication to his mission, and that of our company, to help the war effort of the Republic of South Vietnam in its struggle against Communism, will not be forgotten.

On behalf of Atlantic Architect & Engineers, we offer sincere condolences to you and your family. Please rest assured that you can be proud of your husband's service. He will be missed by all of us.

Most respectfully,

Kevin D. Garsten
Head of Security
AA&E, Area 208 Depot

William M. Posey
Chief of Security
AA&E Inc., Republic of South Vietnam

When he finished the letter, Mike said, "If your dad had been in the service, he probably would have been up for a Bronze or Silver Star."

"Yeah, maybe," Jake agreed. "But there's nothing in place to honor people like him. Just because he wasn't a uniformed soldier doesn't mean that he wasn't a hero, too."

Jake lifted his beer in a toast and clinked with Jenny and Mike's raised bottles.

Epilogue

Mai arrived back in Saigon and had to walk the long distance, in the daytime heat, from the bus station to her room on Nguyen Trai Street. She had no money left for a taxi or pedicab. She was disheveled, distraught, and in need of nourishment, although she had no appetite for food.

The word had gone out in the Tu Do bar area about the shooting. Mai's friend, Phan, who worked at the London bar, soon heard all about it, and had been stopping by Mai's room occasionally, hoping to find her. Just hours after Mai returned, Phan showed up again, and immediately took to caring for her friend. She helped her to bathe and change her clothes, then brought her a bowl of *pho* from the noodle shop below. Mai was so upset that Phan decided to stay for a while; besides, she wanted a break from the London.

After two days, Mai began to talk. Her remorse was overwhelming, but she knew she couldn't change what she'd done. She told Phan that she loved Kendell, and was willing to accept his flaws in hope of a better future. She was willing to deal with his drinking and gambling, even his occasional straying for sex, but she wasn't prepared for the shock and humiliation of being suddenly tossed out like a street girl that someone had just had their way with. What she had done was spontaneous, in the midst of anger and disappointment and rejection.

Phan brought Mai to a Buddhist temple, where she prayed and made offerings in atonement. She spoke to a venerated monk, who told her that the path to redemption was to strive to be an honest, wiser, and better human being, and that she must not give up, because her son and aging parents depended on her.

They came out of the temple and Mai told Phan that she had to work again. She was desperate and broke, but she couldn't go back to Mimi's or anywhere around there because of what had happened. Everyone knew; she couldn't face them. Phan suggested that Cholon might be a better choice.

Cholon was the hub of Chinese commerce in Saigon. It had big, flashy nightclubs where the rich Chinese-Vietnamese went at night. Mai knew about one of them, the Arc En Ciel, so she went there and applied to be a hostess.

She started work the next evening, wearing the Chinese *cheongsam* dress with high heels and makeup. The club had a live band, playing mostly ballroom music, and Mai had to dance with the patrons, who paid for this by the hour. She'd sit with the businessmen, who would buy drinks for her almost non-stop, which boosted her income, and she'd usually try to get the attention of the older men, who always tipped generously. One elderly Chinese man, Mr. Chow, came there almost every night to dance with her, spending lavishly. He was fascinated with her, but never asked to take her out.

Soon enough, Mai was saving a little money. She repaid Phan, who had spent her own money taking care of Mai, and she sent money to her parents in Dong Ha. She wasn't happy, but was doing what needed to be done.

After some weeks working in Cholon, Mai realized that she had missed her monthly period, and was likely pregnant. It was confirmed, but she continued to work every night at the club until the bulge in her stomach became evident in her tight-fitting dresses. She knew that the old Chinese guys wouldn't buy drinks and show off with a pregnant hostess, so she bound her belly with cloth to conceal it for as long as she could. She told Mr. Chow of her plight, but nothing of Kendell, and, surprisingly, he was very sympathetic. Eventually, her condition became a hindrance, so she gave notice and stopped work. Mr. Chow gave her 500 US dollars and wished her good luck.

Mai gave up her room to Phan – who liked the location and would take over the rent – and, with her savings and few belongings, returned to Dong Ha to her parents and son.

***

On July 7, 1969, at a small midwife clinic in Dong Ha, with her older sister beside her, Mai gave birth to a healthy baby girl. Because of the *giay hong thu* co-habitation document, which she'd held on to, Wade Thomas Kendell was legally recorded on the birth certificate as the baby's father.

The child was named Marie Kendell by her mother.

About the Author

Dave Cassier grew up in the seacoast area of New Hampshire. At the age of eighteen he joined the US Army and spent the last ten months of a three-year stint in Vietnam with a combat unit. The unwelcoming atmosphere for veterans in the USA, at the time of his discharge, compelled him to return to Asia in 1966. He became a civilian contractor in Vietnam, remaining there until 1971. He then worked in the oil exploration industry, and has remained as a contractor in the Asia-Pacific region ever since.

Dave has two married daughters in America, both of them born in Vietnam and relocated to the USA as infants. He also has a son, born in Bali, currently attending university in Jakarta, Indonesia. Dave now resides in Thailand.